CAPTIVATED

CAPTIVATED

TYRANNI THOMAS

Captivated

Copyright 2021 Tyranni Thomas
All Rights Reserved

ISBN- **9798456371133**
Cover design by Pretty in Ink Creations
Editing by Michelle's Edits

The content of this book is protected under Federal Copyright Laws. Any unauthorized use of this material is prohibited. No portion of this book may be reproduced in any form without express written permission from the author.

This is a work of fiction. Names, characters, places, and incidents either are the products of the author's imagination or are used fictitiously. Any resemblance to actual persons, living or dead, businesses, companies, events or locales are entirely coincidental.

DEDICATED TO MY
READERS.

Chapter One

The sheet was drenched in my mother's blood. Her lifeless limbs were sprawled and her vacant blue eyes were still fixed on the screaming infant at her side. The moment the midwife noticed that she was gone, the babe was swaddled and ushered away. Someone pushed on my shoulder, nudging me in an urgent manner. It was useless, my feet were heavier than my heart. I couldn't have moved if my life depended upon it. Tears knotted in the back of my throat, but I was too numb to cry.

There wasn't time for tears. It was too late for that, just like it'd been too late for the midwife. She'd been sent for at the last minute, and her executioner would be summoned in the same fashion.

"Highness, please!" she screamed, reaching out for me as the guards set upon her.

"This way princess." The Cardinal's hollow voice seemed so distant.

I shook when his hands found my shoulders, it was the only defense I had. There was nothing one could do to deter the Cardinal when he'd made his mind up about something.

"See that Princess Lita is returned to her chambers," he continued, in a cold, detached tone. "She is much exhausted and requires her bed."

Several hands fluttered over my back in a maternal fashion. It made my skin crawl. I wanted to shrug them off, but I couldn't. The country's great hope was alive and well. My father had his precious son... and now, the good lord had my mother. It was a tremendous loss and an enormous lesson. One that would stick with me for the rest of my days. My mother's womb and its fruits were cherished, but her place in the royal family had always been a replaceable one.

I didn't know how, but while those ladies in waiting tucked me into bed, I swore to myself that I'd never bear children. I'd never marry. My mother had given the king five daughters, and now a son, let him make his alliances with the others.

Chapter Two
Six Years Later

"It isn't fair!" Brianna fussed for the hundredth time today. She stomped her feet and her face soured.

"Shush, child," Aunt Elizabeth chided, delivering a swat to the back of her perfectly curled hair. "You will ruin your powder frowning, what will your father say?"

Brianna's dark brows collided and for a moment, I thought she'd scrub her face just to make a point. I couldn't blame her; she was fourteen and it was her wedding day.

"It isn't! Why doesn't Lita have to marry?"

I used both hands to press the air down between us in a desperate bid for her to lower her voice. Everyone in the royal chapel would hear her if she carried on much longer. My lack of romantic engagement was already gaining enough attention. I was nineteen, and Brianna wasn't the first sister to have been marched begrudgingly down the aisle before me.

"Enough!" the Cardinal demanded, poking his head through the curtain. "I will beat you myself if you do not stop that incessant whining. Princess Lita, get your sister in order!"

He bugged his beady eyes to emphasize his words and Brianna instantly burst into tears.

"Okay, alright…" I stumbled in an effort to soothe her. I awkwardly wrapped my arm around her tiny shoulders. Hugging people made me queasy, it was something I just didn't do, but I managed to offer her upper arm a few pats. "All will be well."

It was the same thing I'd told Abigail before her. It would all turn out, there was no other option. The bells began to ring and the Cardinal fanned the air, bidding us to hurry. His fancy shoes clicked and clacked all the way up the aisle. For being a holy man, he sure was vain. I followed the sound with my head bowed and my face tight. I didn't dare smile or give any indication toward my thoughts. It was a pious occasion. A royal wedding. Half of Frankfort was here to see it. Indeed, not a seat was spared—villagers and nobles alike were crammed into the chapel.

The bells rang again, and I turned my head in accusation. Surely, Brianna had followed me out. Confusion weighed on my brows when the bells rang a third time despite her very obviously being in place behind me.

"What on—?" I began, only to scream when the doors flew open behind Brianna. It sounded like the gates of hell had been kicked in. Men roared and axes were pounded against shields.

Brianna instinctively ran, as did I. While I made it past her intended, William, she did not. He grabbed her shoulders and threw her back toward the burly axe-men who were invading the cathedral. I gasped past the shock and stumbled blindly but there was nowhere to go. People were hysterically swarming around and those bearded fellows were making short work of hacking at them.

Brianna was stuck in the madness. She ran straight into a full-hearted swing. It doubled her at once. She scarcely made a sound, just a mediocre grunt when the axe was ripped from her gut and she was left to bleed out. My brother tore after her, but he met the same fate.

No one seemed to notice or care. No one except a dark-haired heathen. He looked savage with murderous eyes and blood smeared on his face. He pointed the business end of his axe at the man who had killed my siblings and began to bark in a language that I'd never heard before. It was rough and angry sounding. I should have been running, cowering, but instead, I blankly stared at the pair before me.

"You bastard!" I screamed once the shock wore off and reality caught up with me.

I hurled myself onto their killer's back and pounded his broad shoulders with my fists.

"You killed her. You animal, you killed her!" I repeated until my words blurred and my throat burned.

He slung his arm and I was airborne with no effort at all. I landed on the ground with a dull thud and struggled to draw air for a moment. Each time I inhaled, my lungs spasmed and it felt like nails were being dragged down my throat. Meanwhile, the men had grown quiet. The heathen who had come to my sister's defense was suddenly looking at me in a way that I didn't like. His gaze roamed with a boldness that I wasn't familiar with, and then he did the unthinkable; he stared into my eyes like we were equals. My chest rose and fell in suspense. Something inside me screamed for me to run, but I just didn't have it in me. I was still too numb to serve anyone, myself included.

The axe was hefted again, this time, it pointed at me. He said something on a grunt, but it might as well have been gibberish.

When he repeated himself a bit more

forcefully and waved the axe at me like he had the murderer, I carefully stepped toward him. It truly felt like I was floating, my body had bypassed my brain and was moving of its own accord.

Dreaming. Maybe I was dreaming.

His hand snaked out and claimed my upper arm. It was a quick reality check. I was jerked to my tiptoes and that foul grunting drew the attention of everyone around us. He said a few words, hefting my arm now and then to emphasize whatever threats he was making.

"My... Princess," he slowly enunciated.

It caused me to wince on a smile. It was so bizarre, hearing him honor me after such an entrance.

"Mine!" He growled. As he did so, he twisted and hefted my arm again.

All the color drained from my face. He wasn't honoring me; he was claiming me. The realization hit me just like that axe had Brianna. My stomach churned and my lungs failed me all over again. The moment he'd said his piece, he started dragging me out of the cathedral. I locked my hand around his wrist and fought to free myself. It was little use; it barely even slowed his pace. He was so big and strong compared to me. I'd never even wrestled before. I was a fucking princess, who would have dared!

As I struggled along, I was confronted with the aftermath of the raid. Bodies were strewn everywhere. Children and animals scrambled in the distance. Women were being assaulted right there in the street. It was outright shameful, heathen behavior.

On the way to the city gate, a man with long braided blond hair and rotting teeth grabbed my other arm, causing me to be stretched between the two men. My captor refused to stop. He gave my arm another jerk, shearing the other man's grip down the length of my upper arm.

"Ow!" I shrieked in protest.

I flailed between them, not really caring who won the tug of war as long as they stopped trying to tear me in two.

I was flung again, and just like the last time, I landed hard on the pavement. My palms bit the stones, and pain shot through my knees.

The exchange before me sounded violent. The men were nose to nose with their eyes locked and their weapons drawn. Alas, the man with the rotten teeth held his hands up in surrender. He backed away without incident and disappeared into the crowd leaving me with my original captor.

I shivered in the cold, saltwater breeze and my teeth chattered. He didn't leave me to suffer long. My dark-haired captor reached for me. When I leaned into his grip rather than fight him, his gaze softened a bit. My heart raced as we stared into each other's eyes for a moment. It was hard to do, I had to force myself not to avert my eyes. I felt bared before him, I'd never been at someone else's mercy before. The longer he stared, the more I shivered. Alas, he jerked me toward him and hefted me over his shoulder.

My whole world went upside down, I couldn't help but give a short scream. His large hand rested against my hip and much to my disgust, it slid up and down the length of my leg rubbing in a familiar way. The only thing remotely tolerable about it was the way it kept me warm.

I had no idea how long he'd been carrying me, but now that I was paying attention, I realized that sand was being tossed with each of his steps.

This big bastard was trying to get me across the beach!

I whipped left and right, and looked over my shoulder, taking in the scene before me as best as I could. Women and goods were being lugged onto a slew of ships that had little dragon heads etched into the hull.

I began to violently twist and squirm. I couldn't leave. I couldn't be claimed. My destiny was here, in Frankfort! My father had promised me so, and now this oversized fool was trying to fumble and steal me away like the crown jewels.

Well, he wouldn't get them that easy!

He began to bark and stumble, his large hands crashing down on my legs in an effort to still me. We were both screaming and snarling right there in the sand. The men around us roared with laughter. Even a few women on the ships were pointing and smiling with amusement.

"Let me be!" I demanded, with a shove.

It didn't move him an inch. His big hazel eyes were locked on me and his expression was deadly.

"I am Princess Lita of Frankfort and you will stand aside." I lifted my chin and fought the tears that burned the corner of my eyes.

He was going to kill me; I just knew it.

"My Princess," he repeated, stepping into my space once again. He grabbed for my wrist and whipped me back to his side with no effort at all. He was so strong and his body so hard. He pinned me against his side, and his hand roamed the small of my back until a handful of ass was claimed.

I promptly slapped his face, causing another round of laughter.

"Damn you. Damn you all!" I wasn't good at sounding tough let alone cursing. It wasn't often people dared to offend or ridicule me. In fact, it had never happened before.

My captor didn't budge. His grip on my ass remained and so did his smile.

"Mine," he repeated while bringing his mouth dangerously close to my face.

I swallowed, unsure of how long I'd draw air. Tears spilled, carrying my pride and future down my cheeks.

He stepped back and he raised his palm in an unmistakable request.

"You are his, whether you like it or not," a woman from a nearby boat called. Her accent was sultry and foreign, yet she spoke the common tongue. "Best to go without further bloodshed, hmm?"

I shook my head. I wasn't going anywhere.

"Think carefully, lass," she called, with a nod toward some helpless woman in the distance. The poor thing was surrounded by men who were grabbing at her and shearing her clothing. I shivered and sniffled, trying my best to look everywhere, but at that extended hand. He gave a warning grunt and I closed my eyes, shoving my hand out to his with a strangled sob.

Chapter Three

He was a heathen, and yet, he hadn't dishonored or slain me. It went against everything that the Cardinal and tutors had ever taught us about his kind. His hair was tangled and decorated, but his touch, as long as I was compliant, was relatively gentle. I was confused beyond belief, and the rocking of the waves was making me nauseous.

I couldn't stop shaking. Who knew if it was from the cold or my nerves and the uncertainty? The water kept slopping over the side of the boat and the clouds grew angrier above us.

"Lucky for you, we don't go far," the woman with the accent called from her boat. It was keeping time with the one I was riding on. Despite her efforts, I remained quiet. In truth, I was afraid I'd be sick if I opened my mouth for any reason at all.

Her words should have been a comfort. We weren't going far! That meant that I'd have less ground to travel home when I escaped, but all of that went right over my head. All I could focus on was the misery around me. The hem of my gown was sopping wet and mildly discolored. The goosebumps on my arms and the churning in my gut were enough to make me want to pass out. Those were the things I had to conquer first. If I ever managed to get them under control, then I might worry about small talk.

"Princess." My captor reached out and touched my cheek before rumbling off a bunch of gibberish. I tried to dismiss it as such, but he quickly pulled my face back toward his.

"He is oathing you stars and moon." The woman in the boat next to me smiled.

"He can keep them!" I spat without thinking.

Luckily, he didn't seem to have a clue what

I had said. He kept on smiling and staring at me. His palm stroked my cheek and then came to rest on my shoulder.

"Mine," he repeated, on a sigh.

"Where are you taking me?" I whispered, staring down at his hand.

He abruptly looked toward the woman in the boat and spoke to her. All I could do was look between them and curse myself for not learning enough languages. Not that it mattered, the tutors didn't teach heathen speak. No one did. It was uncivilized and likely a language of the damned.

I realized that I was frowning and that they were both staring at me.

"He said he is taking you to your new home," the woman offered. "He said I am to serve you both now."

She said it so calmly. *Serve*. It was a simple word and yet I understood. She was to be his slave, or perhaps she already was. I frowned more and took it all in, keeping a sharp eye on my captor. I instinctively leaned away from him every time he so much as breathed too heavily.

"Where is home? Where are you taking me?" I spoke to him now, fully expecting his slave to interpret now that I knew what she was.

She didn't disappoint. Their harsh language flowed around me and after a time, she announced, "North Frankfort."

I blinked and glanced back over my shoulder in the direction of the Frankfort shore. It was a sizable country sure, but why wouldn't they sail back to their own land? Why risk staying and losing their plunder?

"You will all die," I predicted.

"No. They will thrive under new Treaty of William." She beamed.

There was at least four yards between our boats, and yet it felt like she'd struck me.

The Treaty of William?

All I could picture was William flinging Brianna toward her murderer. It suddenly made sense. My world started to spin and my legs went weak. I landed against what may as well have been a tree trunk. Of course, it was only my captor. His eager hands wrapped around me and held me snug against him once more.

"Who are you?" I mumbled, quietly.

He grunted at the girl in the other boat, but she offered nothing in return.

"Does he have a name?" I asked somewhat louder. "Am I allowed to know who has taken me hostage?"

She laughed and they exchanged a few words around me again.

"His name is Ozias. He is husband, you are not hostage," she corrected, in her broken way.

"Ow-Zigh As." I repeated, feeling ever so dumb. It sounded foreign and odd. I was certain I'd butchered it. You wouldn't have known it from looking at him though, his smile was so proud.

Everything was hitting me at once. The loss of my siblings. The betrayal. It almost escaped me that she had said something about a husband.

Almost.

"What did you just say?" I squinted toward her, completely dismissing the oversized Viking to my right.

"You did well. Yes, Ozias." She nodded.

"No. I get it, his name is Ozeus… Oziah…. Ozzy, damn it. What did you just say about a husband?"

"Oh." She beamed and bobbed her head again, "Ozias is husband now. You are no hostage. You are wife."

My gown was drenched to the knee and my toes were pruned in my socks from the quarter inch of water that was sloshing about in the bottom of the boat. The waves were relentless. A storm was brewing out at sea and part of me prayed for it to take me. I didn't want to be his prisoner. I didn't want to be his princess. And I, damn sure, didn't want to be his wife.

I didn't think. I didn't even breathe. I just turned and shoved. The splash that Ozias made on the other side of the boat sent chills through me. What had I done? Now I was alone with them! The men who had been doing all those terrible, disgusting things to the women back in my palace. I tore air into my lungs so hard and fast it hurt and hurled myself over the edge.

Chapter Four

The water was so cold that I screamed the moment I plunged into it. Water filled my lungs and there was no way to sputter. The surface grew further and further away. I flailed and desperately tried to swim my way to the top, but no one had ever taught me how. Such things weren't meant for royal ladies. My mind was in overdrive, and then, like a candle being blown out everything shut off.

The fight left me. The fear melted and I was alone with my thoughts.

I was going to die.

Something caught my peripherals. It moved fast and tread the sea without effort. It had to be a creature. A shark or some predator that had come to end it.

It hooked around my middle and tore me

back toward the surface so fast that the panic came back to me. I started to fight, but all that left me the moment we broke through. I sputtered violently and my lungs spasmed for air. Pain rocked my chest and I instantly burst into tears.

Ozias held onto my middle and made soothing noises against my ear. The burning in my chest was so fierce, all I could do was cling to him and heave.

I must have blacked out. The next thing I knew my underarms were being wrenched and I was hauled from the icy water. I'd gotten used to it, until they flung me to the bottom of the ship. A large man with a braided beard kicked me in the stomach while the others concentrated on getting Ozias back on board.

I couldn't even cry out properly, my coarse sounds were more akin to a wounded seal than a lady.

Ozias barked a single word and the man with the beard stopped mid-kick. He lowered his boot and glared back, but he didn't utter a word. I wanted to ask the slave if Ozias was in charge, but I doubted she'd be able to hear or understand me. So, I lay down on the boat, as near to that filthy water as I could and tried to keep the wind off of me. I was so drenched I doubted anyone could see my tears, but Ozias did. He snagged my shoulders, rocked me into a sitting position and lifted me to his lap without a word.

He was as wet as I was. I was the one who had tossed him in, and yet his arms wrapped around me and started to strum my side in an effort to keep me warm. It was too much. I didn't know if my father was alive or dead. It was hard telling if my kingdom even knew that I was kidnapped, and to top all of that off, the man I needed to hate was doing everything in his heathen power to comfort me.

I wanted to scream, or cry, or tear his beautiful green eyes out, but instead I just huddled on his lap like a doll and let the tears roll. He swiped them away at first, but after a time he gave up and let me pour it all out on his shoulder.

I desperately wanted a last glance at my kingdom, but I soon learned that it didn't take long for a coast to disappear. It brought another bout of tears and a nauseating round of helplessness. A large fur was thrown over us and his arms shifted about only to swaddle me again. The slave in the other boat was glaring at me, I felt it long before I found her dark, beady eyes cutting my way.

"You are foolish, spoiled girl!" she shouted when she caught me looking. "He is bravest amongst them. You nearly ruin it for both of us."

I said nothing. Hell, I was so spent, I didn't even flinch when she spat into the water between us.

"Three years I serve Ozias. I do not know hunger. No trouble come my way. I know peace and stability only under Ozias. You ignorant girl," she rattled, until Ozias growled something.

A tall, tattooed man with a massive axe stepped forward and struck her in the mouth. Her head and hair flew, but she didn't make a sound. She was bold and fixed that same glare on the man who had assaulted her. She looked to the ground with contempt. I could tell she was thinking about spitting again, but in the end, she turned and walked away.

"Forgive...," he whispered against my ear.

It sent a chill through me. I instinctively threw my shoulder toward my ear and whipped about to face him better. Had I truly heard him? Maybe it was just a word that sounded like one I recognized.

"Slave. Only slave," he furthered.

It wasn't what he said, it was how he said it. The words were few, but his eyes swung around like he was paranoid.

"You can speak my language?" I gasped, only for his hand to clamp over my mouth.

He shook his head in denial, and looked past me toward the waves.

"Little. Very little." His tone was so deep, it drew me in.

"But you understand what I'm saying?" I leaned forward, half wanting to slap him for making me speak through the interpreter.

His head bobbled in a half-hearted nod.

"Some," he admitted, finally meeting my gaze.

"You're not my husband," I flatly informed him.

He flashed a smile that could have made a whore blush and licked his lips. "In North Frankfort, I am."

Fire flew through me. It ignited my hand before I could even realize that I'd aimed it at that face of his. It connected with a satisfying sound. He winced, but the smile remained. The men around us were now openly gawking. Some were laughing and others spoke in bawdy tones.

"My Princess," he told the crowd rather than me.

"No." I set my jaw.

He sniffed and looked away, that infuriating smile ever present.

Chapter Five

The last few hours were insufferable. I squirmed. I sighed. I felt like Abigail and Brianna with the number of times I rolled my eyes and sulked. There was nothing I could do; I was at his mercy and clearly the best source of amusement on the ship. It was better to remain quiet than entertain the lot of them.

Someone nudged Ozias and spoke in the heathen tongue. He immediately tapped my leg and stood, leaving me scrambling to find my feet.

"What?" I panicked, half hoping it was a shore full of my father's men.

"Home." He pointed to the deserted beach.

Not only was the beach empty, so were the hills around it. There were no warning fires. Even the towers were vacant of any signs of life. My heart stopped. At least I thought it had, the way my head went light and I couldn't draw air.

I regained consciousness on the back of Ozias' shoulder. Our near-death experience seemed to have been nothing to him. He hauled me to the sand and plopped me down on my backside. It rattled me a bit and I cried out from the impact.

"North Frankfort." The slave smiled, some two feet from me. Her bare feet were covered in sand granules, and her dirty hands were reaching out to help me. I cringed, but took them all the same. She none too gently jerked me to my feet and then dusted her hands off like I'd contaminated them. I curled my fists, but Ozias bumped my upper arm hard enough to bruise me. The sad part was he seemed to have only meant to nudge me. I had to get away from this big brute and all his heathen friends.

Even if he was the bravest of them, whatever that meant.

The wind blew, reminding me that I was

soaked and miserable. My shoes were ruined and my stockings were squishy. I just wanted a hot bath and my bed. I wanted to be home where things were normal. If I could only go back to last night and sneak us all away. Brianna must have begged me to do so a half dozen times. Instead, I followed Ozias and the slave through the countryside. We arrived at a small farm and separated from the others. It was half dilapidated and more than a little creepy-looking. While we made our way to the front door, the others traipsed on toward the houses in the distance.

"Don't kill them," I hurriedly begged, only to be rewarded with a bizarre look from the slave.

"Death would be mercy. They live only to die. No battle in them," the slave lectured.

Ozias threw the door open and held it until the slave and I had passed. Luckily, the house was already vacant. Whoever lived there had likely ran when they saw the heathens coming. I prayed so, anyhow.

While Ozias and I stood there and stared at

one another, the slave huffed and moved off to stoke the fire. I stared at her, unsure of what I should be doing.

"Truth takes care of us," he said, and his finger slid along my cheek. I darted my head back to avoid his touch and he laughed.

"Truth?"

"The slave." He nodded toward her. "Names Truth. She doesn't lie, even when she should."

I watched her sniff at a pot and position it over the flames. It made my stomach churn; she didn't know how long that had been hanging there. Suppose it had insects in it or mold? My stomach flopped and my mouth watered. I sprinted toward the door and vomited just beyond it. Ozias was hot on my heels. I think he thought I was going to run, but I couldn't have if I wanted to. My feet were still water logged and the rest of me wasn't faring much better. I held onto the door frame until I was white knuckled and my stomach had settled.

"I need to sleep," I announced.

"Sleep?" he repeated, his brows furrowing a bit.

"Yes, preferably in a bed!" I snapped, without meaning to.

"Bed!" He recognized that word and waved me toward the back of the house. In a little room off a short hallway, was a bed. It was just a straw-stuffed mattress and a blanket, but it would do. Provided he left me alone. I stared at him for a good long while, neither of us blinking. My heart started to race and I wondered if he would leave me or insist on joining me.

Alas, he turned and made his way back toward Truth leaving me to my thoughts. There were too many of them. All the worry and replaying of events wouldn't fix anything. I stretched out on the mattress only to toss and turn every time I fell asleep. Of course, my eyes shot open a few minutes later in a state of panic.

About the third time it happened, I woke on a gasp and realized there were noises coming from the other room. A faint scraping sound and moaning sifted through the hall. It sent chills through me. I threw my legs quietly from the bed and padded to the door. My heart was slamming in my chest as I tilted just a bit to see around the bend.

My eyes bugged when I found Truth spread out on the kitchen table. Her naked form slithered and ground against Ozias. My mouth fell open, but I didn't dare say anything. I scampered back to bed and stared at the door. The sounds went on forever and part of me wanted to use the opportunity to sneak out of my window, but I was afraid. What if I drew attention? What if he then tried to do those sinful things to me? I shivered and pulled the covers up to my neck. Let them rut until the cows came home, I decided at least it meant his attention wasn't on me.

Still, I tossed and turned. What did it mean? Why would he insist that he was my husband and then do… that? I glanced toward the window and my mind once again wandered with thoughts of running.

A loud bang nearly made me cry out, but I managed to hitch and hold my breath instead. A few minutes passed with me straining to hear, then footsteps started to approach. I clamped my eyes shut and clutched the blanket to my chin.

The steps came closer, and then the straw mattress shifted beneath his weight. A large arm wrapped around me and I was pulled toward him rather forcefully. My back abruptly met his chest and I huffed out the breath I'd been holding.

"Sleep," he mumbled against the crook of my neck. His body was slick with sweat and sticking to mine. I wanted to wiggle my shoulders and demand some space, but I didn't dare risk inspiring him. I lay awake and as still as a corpse until the sun peeked through the window.

It was so gross. I couldn't even think about it, I just forced myself to focus on one breath and then the next. I fought tears and frustration alike, until I finally could take no more. I threw the covers back and started to fling my legs over the edge of the mattress. On the way to do so, however, I caught sight of him. His large naked frame. He seemed oblivious to the fact that I'd bared him, and I couldn't drag my eyes away. I'd never seen a man naked before. His chest might as well have been carved. There was no soft middle, his belly was hard and tight. Then my eyes sank to his cock and I gasped. It was hard and staring at me. That was when I realized he was, too. That stupid smile of his was stretched across his face and his eyes were more than suggestive.

I backhanded him hard on the shoulder and he laughed like I was the cutest thing in the kingdom. He reached out and swooped me up again, hauling me to that broad chest of his.

"My Princess," he purred against my ear.

All those muscles and that girthy cock of his was flushed against my back. I panicked and flailed, catching him in the nose with an elbow. He released me at once and clutched it between steepled hands.

"Stay away from me!" I warned, as sternly

as I dared.

I whipped around to face him and Truth snatched both my arms and pinned them behind me.

"He is husband. He does what he wants!" she barked in my ear.

Ozias raised his hand and grunted.

Truth started to yell at him in that unfamiliar tongue and he shot off the bed and started to yell right back. She cowered and left the room, but not before affording me a glare.

Chapter Six

"Come," he mumbled, wrapping a fur around his shoulders. He didn't even bother to hide his shame, he just left it dangling and took off in an expectant manner.

"Take fur so you have something to dry with," Truth huffed, but at least had enough respect to avert her scornful gaze.

She rolled her lips, and I could tell she was about to spit again, but her eyes lifted and met Ozias's at the last minute and she decided against it. She grabbed a fur from the back of a chair and shoved it into my arms.

"Come," Ozias repeated, and took a hold of my arm.

He didn't pull me; I didn't give him a chance to. I hurried after him, not willing to risk my dignity with any public displays. We went behind the house and down a hill. There was a creek with clear water and smooth stones in the bottom. It was as cold as ever, but the water was cleaner than the seaweed we'd waded in through. I took off my stockings and stepped inside. I'd almost forgotten Ozias was there. Until I looked past the ankle I was scrubbing and realized he was squatting beside me bathing himself without a care in the world.

"What's wrong with you?" I spat turning on him.

It had only been an ankle, but still. Didn't he know what the word privacy meant?

"Bathe," he said, in a way that was a bit too firm to have been a suggestion.

"I'm not Truth. I'm no slave for you to order about. I'm Lita of Frankfort. Princess. Eldest daughter of King Charles."

He stared at me with amusement shining in his eyes. I tried to shove him, but he caught my wrist and spun me around.

"Bathe," he repeated, while hauling the hem of my gown up my knees.

I wasn't having a bit of it. I fought him until we were both on our backs and wrestling in the rocks. He was stronger, though. The big buffoon sat on top of me and peeled my dress off without a single apology. While I curled up and covered what I could, he splashed water on me and rubbed my back.

I jerked away from him when I could and even tried to bite him once. I'm sure he was ready to hurt me, but he never did. He had the patience of a saint, and I hated him all the more for it.

When he'd finished, he grabbed the fur and stood in front of me with the thing spread open like an invitation. I wanted to deny it, but I knew that would leave me walking back naked. So, I stood up and gave him my back. He blanketed me in the fur and grabbed his own.

"Come." He nodded.

"You're a great conversationalist. What do

you suppose we will do for the rest of our days, grunt at each other?" I raged and shivered behind him.

"There's plenty of time for us to do that." He winked, and I felt my whole face flush.

"Shush!" I demanded, taking a swat at him.

He dodged it and laughed. He wasn't ugly. His laughter was pure and he wasn't the worse personality I'd ever suffered. It would have been easy to allow myself to fall into line, but I couldn't. I wasn't a heathen. I didn't live in the forest and worship demons and devils, or whatever they did. I recalled tales from the castle of sacrifices and dancing under the moon. It made me hurry back to the house a little faster.

I couldn't allow myself to be lost in thoughts. I had to figure out what was going on with my father and our people. He quick stepped beside me and reached for the door just as I arrived.

"How long do you think it will be before a counter attack is laid?" I asked, slamming my hand on the door.

It snapped shut and he jerked his fingers back like I'd caught them, but I was pretty sure I'd missed, just barely. He stared at me like I was half mad and sucked on a knuckle.

"My people will come for me," I simplified.

"Your people?" he repeated, his brows lifting a bit. "They are King William's people now."

He reached for the door like the conversation was over, but I planted my hand on it again and cocked my head so that he had to look at me.

"I need to see my father, Ozias. Please..." I didn't have to pretend, my lip quivered and my heart stilled a bit.

"You need to accept your new life." He grabbed my wrist and removed it from the door.

"Ozias..." The word broke in my throat. "Please."

I'd never begged anyone in my life. I felt so small. He looked into my eyes and paused a moment, his chin lifting like he was encouraging me to do the same.

"Your father is dead."

"You saw him fall?" I demanded.

His brows dipped and he shook his head in denial.

"I know as a warrior, that if I were King William, I would slay him first or as soon as I was able." He shrugged like it was a common strategy. "There cannot be three kings."

This time it was my turn to be dumbfounded. I stared blankly at him and repeated, "Three kings?"

He grunted in confirmation.

"What three kings? King Charles is the one and only true King of Frankfort."

"King Charles the Fallen, King William the Brave, and King Ozias of North Frankfort." He confidently informed me.

"You mean William the Pretender, Ozias the Coward, and my father. The one true king!" I spat.

He inhaled ever so slowly and reached toward me. I wasn't quick enough to dodge him, that large palm spanned the back of my head and he pulled me in for a slow kiss. My cheeks flooded with shame and I brought my hand up to smack him, but he was once again quicker. He pinned me and smothered my mouth with his. There was no hiding, his lips nipped at mine and his tongue trailed my lower lip until I bit him.

His calloused hand found my throat and I stilled. My heart slammed in my chest and my eyes locked with his.

"Stop…" It almost sounded like he was pleading. Then his hand gave my throat a little hug and his lips pressed against the top of my head. It was possessive and protective all wrapped into one.

Laughter brewed behind him, and I squirmed away just enough to see a man with long blond braids watching us.

"Brother, I think she bested you," he said, much more fluently than Ozias.

Ozias grunted and said something to the man in his native tongue, but the man kept right on using English.

"Your new shield maiden or another slave?" His gaze crawled over me. There was nothing I could do to avoid it, the fur simply didn't reach all the way around me, so I wrapped it under my arm and left a thigh sticking out.

"My wife," Ozias corrected.

"'Wife.'" His brother chuckled and shook his head. "What business have you with a wife?"

"She will win the people. My new people. Sven, stop with so many questions. Come, sup with us." Ozias opened the door and locked his gaze on me. "Get dressed and stop embarrassing me."

He swatted me hard on the bottom when I passed, catching the still damp flesh of my hip. It left little lines where his fingers had landed and irked me to no end. I wanted to hurt him, but I had to keep moving or risk another blow to my dignity. I knew I couldn't best him and it was probably in my best interest not to try with an audience.

Chapter Seven

That night the moaning started again, only this time, I could hear Sven growling and grumbling in passion right along with them. It made me want to be sick, or perhaps I was just so upset because I didn't feel nauseated by the things they were doing. Was Ozias really in there participating in those sinful acts? I crept to the bedroom door and watched the shadows playing out on the wall. The contortion acts and bouncing curves.

Truth was overly loud, making certain that I would hear them.

She leaned back, making a bow of a figure on the wall. I was so captivated watching it, that I didn't realize Ozias was standing at the end of the hall.

"You want to join?" he asked, with a sweaty smile.

I shut the door in his face and went to hide in the bed. He was unmoved by the display, and opened the door right behind me. It made me regret coming to the bed at all. The only comfort I found in being in the same room with him, was the fact that he had his britches on. It was a short-lived mercy, he jerked them off his hips and joined me like it was a natural occurrence.

I nearly slid right off my side of the bed, and would have if he wasn't quick enough to capture my arm and haul me against him. My shift caught against his naked body and I gasped.

"No!" I couldn't believe how firm I sounded.

It seemed to shock him, too. His shoulders relaxed, but his hands remained behind me, having locked on my waist.

"You must learn to love me," he whispered, so close that I could feel his warm breath.

Love led to babies. Babies led to death. And I wasn't about to suffer my mother's fate.

"No," I repeated, while trying to pull away from him.

His hand planted just above my knee and shifted up my thigh, carrying the thin material with it.

"Stop!" I insisted, giving a kick.

He blocked it just in time, but at least he let go of me.

"You're curious..." he accused.

"I'm not!" I hissed with a bit of venom. "What they are doing is a sin. You will all go to Hell for this."

"Is that what they do in your Hell?" he asked, with a lewd smile.

"Go to bed." I meant to demand it, but a bit it came off a little pleading.

"Goodnight, my princess."

He tugged me back into place against his front. I twisted about and gave him my shoulder. I couldn't stand that smile, not for one more second. To top matters, I was so exhausted from not sleeping the night before, that I completely passed out. He was still holding me when the birds started chirping and the light trickled through the bedroom window.

He must have been pretty tired, too; he didn't even wake up when I lifted his arm and slid from the bed. The house was eerily silent. Even Truth was still tangled up with Sven and sleeping. Her lips were parted and the tiniest of snores were coming from her.

My mind started to race and I realized, this was my chance. I tiptoed toward the door and opened it carefully. I winced when the thing creaked, but thankfully, no one noticed. The sunlight kissed my cheeks, and the birds were singing. It was a beautiful morning.

I knew there were neighbors, but I couldn't see them from the position of the house. It wasn't until I braved the first hill that I saw two farmhouses below. They were scattered enough that I thought I could pass through unnoticed. I kept to the shrubs and hurried along. Everyone was doing their chores and busying themselves. No one could say these folks were lazy, I'd give them that.

Their work kept them occupied long enough for me to get a few miles down the road. I wondered how far I would make it before Ozias realized I was gone. The thought made me move all the quicker. My calves soon hurt and I was greedily gasping for air. I hadn't realized I was running, but sure enough, I was skirting through the forest. If I could just find the river, I could follow it south. The problem was, I was so eager to hear it I kept mistaking every little sound for the rush of water.

Soon, the birds stopped singing their morning song and the noon sun was high above me. I was turned around and lost. The only thing I seemed to be able to find were the damned sticker bushes.

Day faded to evening, and the sun started to set. The temperature had already dropped, and I knew I'd be in trouble if I didn't find shelter soon. What was I thinking? I didn't even have the means to start a fire. I groaned and rubbed my face. There was a large bush that had some branches hanging over. It might have made a good den for deer. Unfortunately, it was the only thing remotely promising.

My belly growled and I placed my hands over it like I had the power to shush it. Of course, it kept right on rumbling. I started to shiver and cursed the fact that all I'd worn was a shift. No matter how far past my knees I tried to pull it, I was still miserable and exposed. In the end, I pulled my knees to my chest and shrugged the shift down to my ankles. I couldn't move. I wasn't comfortable, but at least the chill was off my legs for the moment.

"Lee-tah," a voice called from the distance.

It was hard to tell which way it had come from with all the echoing of the forest. Chills ran through me and I scrambled about in my den, unsure of where to go or what to do. I didn't know how Ozias would react to my disappearing, and though I was lost, it was still better than being captive.

"There you are," someone closer scoffed.

I whipped around and came face to face with Truth. Her eyes glistened with amusement and a smile split her features.

"Go away," I pleaded.

She gave a nod and looked me up and down.

"My pleasure," she coldly agreed, before stomping past the den and shouting as if she had never seen me, "Lita!"

Something shifted rather abruptly and the limbs were cast away from me. I knew it was Ozias even if it happened too fast for me to see him. He snatched a hold of me and dragged me from the den. Instinct left me grappling, but there was nothing but grass to grab onto and it just didn't hold up against that heathen.

I was hauled on my belly across the ground and flipped over to face him.

"You!" He angrily shook his head. I could tell he wanted to say more but was unable to find the words he wanted.

"You are stupid girl. Place self in danger.

Completely selfish, make husband chase you. King William will kill you." Truth spat at my feet.

Ozias turned on her, but she was already hopping back like she expected a reaction from him.

"You mustn't seek to provoke things," He agreed. "William will kill you."

I looked between their moonlit faces, searching for something more.

"What makes you so sure that William is King and not my father?" I demanded. "What makes you think that he would dare risk offending me or my family?"

Ozias stared at me like I was the simplest thing on the planet. They knew something that I didn't, and I didn't like it one little bit.

Chapter Eight

The walk home was a long one. I supposed that's how defeat usually worked. My scowl had grown so that I couldn't help the weight of my brow or the thinness of my lips. All I could do was glare when we returned home and Sven was still drinking at the table. I made my way through the kitchen and started to pass him, but Ozias reached for me.

I stilled and jerked my arm away before he could take hold of me again.

"Sit," he commanded. "Listen."

Sven's baby-blue eyes shifted from me to Ozias and back again. Then they spoke in their native language and left me in the dark for a time. With a sigh, I relented and sat down in a chair.

"He wants me to explain a few things to you," Sven finally announced, looking my way.

I rolled my eyes and afforded him a patronizing smile.

"Well, by all means, let's hear it."

"William has your father. He doesn't know what to do with him, so he is holding him prisoner," Sven said matter-of-factly.

"That's not true," I interrupted almost inaudibly.

"It is true. He is afraid to kill him, and yet, he is afraid to set him free," Ozias furthered.

"He can't do that." My temper got away from me and I stood up from my seat. "He cannot hold the king hostage. We must..." I trailed off realizing there was no 'we.' What did they care if my father was tortured or killed? It would serve them in the end.

"What, princess?" Ozias studied me and reached out for my cheek.

I tilted my face away from him and ground my teeth.

"You want me to get him?" Ozias asked, with an odd look in his eye.

My breath caught and I held his gaze for a while, unwilling to beg and terrified not to.

"Please...," I finally managed.

"Why?" He shrugged, "Why should I do this thing for you?"

Indignation washed through me and I felt my cheeks flush with anger.

"Because he is your king!" I spat, before I could realize it wasn't true.

"You are my princess," Ozias corrected. "The King means nothing to me. Another man to sit around and get fat while his people starve."

I wanted to argue with him; to counter the things he was saying about my father, but I knew better. Not if I wanted his help.

"If you do it, I will be your wife," I whispered.

Ozias's eyes swung toward his brother and they mumbled back and forth a bit.

"No," Truth interjected.

Ozias' hand raised to silence her without even looking her way.

"You will be my wife," he slowly enunciated. "Only then will I seek vengeance on your behalf."

I felt small and at a disadvantage, but what more did I have to bargain with? It was all he wanted from me. A princess to call his own. And it was clear that he would have it. At least this way I had some type of say in the matter.

"I want a wedding," I piped up. "With a priest."

"A priest?" Sven busted out laughing.

"Then you shall have one," Ozias agreed, causing Sven to grow quiet. He had a scar beneath his eye that twitched with annoyance.

"She is yours. You do not need some holy

man to deem it so, brother."

Truth snorted and Ozias slapped his hands on the table.

"Enough. It is my decision," he reminded them, before giving me his attention once more. "And I have chosen the princess. Whatever makes her happy... so shall it be."

The room filled with a heavy silence, then Ozias reached out and slid a tendril of my hair behind my ear.

"Come. Let us talk. Alone." He glanced between his brother and his slave.

He took my hand and gently led me toward the bedroom. It was perhaps the first time I wanted to be behind closed doors with him.

"How do I know you won't trick me, and leave my father to rot after I exchange vows with you?" I panicked, once we were inside.

He raised his arm and touched the band that lay above his wrist.

"Because I oath my loyalty to you, once we are married."

He said it like it held the same weight as swearing on the bible. Perhaps in his world it did.

Chapter Nine

He led me to a small desk in the corner of the room and pilfered around until he found a piece of parchment and some ink.

"What is this?" Confusion kept my voice low and my brows knitted.

"For you to make the treaty." He nodded.

"What treaty?"

"The treaty of marriage. Isn't that what your people do? You write things down and it becomes magically legal?" He waved the quill in front of me.

"Yes... no. I mean sometimes. Marriage isn't like that. Marriage requires a priest. A ceremony. Happiness..." My voice trailed off as I ventured into hopeful waters.

"I will make you happy," he said, with a bit of conviction.

I didn't know how to answer him, so I just stayed quiet.

"Where do we find this... priest?" He acted like the word was a hard one to swallow.

"I don't imagine you travel with one, huh?" I laughed at myself before sobering with realization. "We will likely be hard pressed to find one that hasn't fled south."

"Sven," he called, causing me to jump a bit.

Bootsteps proceed Sven's appearance at the door. He sort of draped himself against the side of it and stared at us. Amusement was rife in his eyes and he had a smirk that could have competed with Ozias's.

"Yes?"

"Put the word out. I will pay handsomely for a priest."

"What? No!" I stumbled to spit my words out before either of them could act. "You cannot pay someone to kidnap a priest."

It was unthinkable. At least in my world it was, but not theirs. Sven gave a nod and tore off through the house, leaving me to call his name. I couldn't chase him. The minute I turned from the chair, Ozias's hands were at my waist, holding me in place while he made shushing sounds against my ear.

"You want a wedding and a priest. So shall it be."

"I want the priest's blessing. He will excommunicate us both." I desperately tried to reason with him, but it was useless.

"What is... excommunicate?" He tilted his head.

"It means he will curse," Truth taunted from the doorway. "Religious man holds much power in her world."

"No." I spoke over her. "It isn't like that. Stop trying to paint our priests as demons."

"If he curses you, I will kill him," Ozias promised, while gravely staring at me.

"Priests don't curse people. Heathens do!" I pleaded, but he was already walking away.

He and Truth spoke for some time in that language that I couldn't understand. They stood in the corner of the kitchen and kept their voices low. It frustrated me to no end. I couldn't correct the lies she so easily spread and it made me feel so very vulnerable.

"I have other conditions," I said, taking up a seat at the kitchen table.

I tried to pretend like I had a backbone, but the truth was, I'd spent my life being represented. Either by my father or an advocate of his court.

"If I am to marry you, the slave will have to go. I will not share a husband."

Truth's spine went stiff and she turned on her heel and hurled herself at me. Ozias seemed to have lost a few words in translation, but he knew enough to grab for her when she lunged. She scratched and swung at the air while he struggled to hold her.

I kept my head high and my chin parallel to the floor, maintaining a regal posture. I wouldn't be moved by the likes of her.

"Truth is my property—" he began.

"The table is your property, but you do not rut with it," I pointed out. "The hounds and horses..."

I cocked my head as if I were trying to see them out the window.

"You bitch!" Truth cried. She couldn't reach me, so she started to spit all over the floor. It came nowhere near me, so I still remained impassive to her performance.

"Enough!" Ozias barked, delivering a swat to the slave's legs.

She was seething. I could see it in her dark eyes and the way she kept her fists curled tight.

"I will not lie with her," he agreed, once things had quieted.

Truth jerked away from him and ran outside.

"I will not feel safe under the same roof as her," I pushed my luck. "She must be sold."

He sucked air through his teeth, tapped his nails on the table and started back toward the bedroom.

Chapter Ten

Things in the little farmhouse went from bad to worse over the next few days. The only time Truth smiled was when we ate supper. She would stare at me with a malicious grin that often left me wondering if it would be my last meal.

Ozias barely said a word until the night Sven returned. He'd been gone almost a week. I was starting to wonder if he had intentions of coming back at all. The longer things carried on, the more paranoid I became. Nothing was sacred, I suspected everyone and everything. Especially Sven. What if it wasn't even a priest he'd brought back, but some random butcher or a smith?

All those doubts washed away when Sven waved to someone beyond the door and a few of Ozias's men drug the good cardinal inside.

"Unhand me, heathens!" he demanded in that righteous way of his.

His mouth flopped open and his eyes rounded when he saw me.

"Highness," he gasped. "Highness, thank heavens, you're alive."

"Cardinal Tullini," I whispered, unable to believe my eyes.

I was starting to tear up and my breath was hitching as I waited for him to get on with it. Surely, he would tell me of my father's demise.

"Well…?" I asked, after a time of us tearfully gawking at one another. "What of my father. Where is he? How is he?"

He swallowed hard and shifted his gaze toward Ozias. I realized that Ozias hadn't said a word yet. He was rather good at leading people to believe he was ignorant of our ways and language.

"His majesty is being held in the tower. He is fed half rations and allowed no visitors, I'm afraid." The Cardinal clutched the rosary that hung from his wrist and solemnly closed his eyes.

"Then we must act quickly, while he is still alive." I turned toward Ozias and looked up at him. He was so much taller than me, I instinctively placed a hand on his chest to draw his attention.

"Oh. Oh dear." The Cardinal sputtered, staring over at us. He crossed himself and took up his prayer beads again.

I felt ashamed under his judgement and immediately dropped my hand.

"It's okay, Cardinal. He is to be my husband."

My words only served to make the man pale. He crossed himself again and his frown was palpable.

"That is impossible. You are the heir to the Frankfort throne, Highness. You cannot have a... a..." He stuttered a bit and cut his sentence short. "It simply won't do, Princess."

"He is the man who is going to return my father to his throne." I tried to sound final about it, but the Cardinal parted his lips to speak again.

"You have someone else in mind?" Sven spoke up.

Cardinal Tullini clutched his chest and looked pained for a moment.

"Cardinal?" I hurried to his side, but he was reluctant to allow my touch. The man acted like I had the plague for all the show he put into backing away from me.

"God will provide a way." He raised his voice.

"He has," I softly pointed out. "You will wed us, and then Ozias will gather his men on my behalf. The same men who took Frankfort the first time, only now, they will be on our side."

"And then what? Shall we look the other way and pretend they are not murderous heathens?" The Cardinal's cheeks reddened. "What of the lives that were lost?"

"If you refuse, my father's blood will be on your hands." This time I didn't have to pretend, the disgust kept my voice even.

Who was he to deny a royal order? Did he really think himself above my father and family? I was seriously sick of the Cardinal. Why couldn't he just do what he was told?

"You see," Truth muttered. "What did I say about religious man in this country?"

She leaned forward, clearly preparing to spit on the Cardinal, but Ozias was faster. He shot his hand out so that his palm became a muzzle and shoved her head back.

"Marry us and live, Priest," he announced, smacking the table with his other hand.

"Absolutely not," the Cardinal hissed, unmoved by the realization that Ozias could speak English. He wasn't used to ultimatums and Ozias had run out of patience. I felt sick to my stomach and light headed all at once.

"Sven, take him outside," Ozias quietly growled.

"No! Wait," I begged.

My words fell on deaf ears. Sven grabbed the Cardinal by his collar and started jerking him toward the door. When the older man's legs gave out, Sven dragged him through the dirt like a commoner.

I scrambled after them, bumping shoulder-to-shoulder with Truth in the doorway. I shoved her aside and threw myself on Sven.

"Stop, please." He started whipping his arm about, trying to toss me aside. "Sven, please! I implore you, do not hurt him. He is a man of God."

I rambled, desperately searching for something that would make him stop.

"It is a great sin to shed the blood of a holy man. A curse will befall your whole family for generations to come," I lied.

He stilled in his tracks and glared down at Cardinal Tullini.

"Marry them, or I shall strangle you with my bare hands or perhaps I will drown you in the sea... I'm a patient and creative man, Priest," Sven growled.

The Cardinal was gasping and clutching his chest. I thought he might keel over at any minute. Instead, he bobbed his head in agreement and crossed himself from a fetal position.

Chapter Eleven

The Cardinal was taken to a shack out back. Ozias, at my insistence had tasked Truth with providing him a pail of water so that he might freshen up.

When she returned, her eyes were murderous. Ozias barked at her in that harsh-sounding language and it turned into a shouting match. When he locked his jaw and gave her that warning glare, she slunk toward me and sighed dramatically.

"Come. I get you ready for wedding."

She let herself into our bedroom and started rummaging through the closet. She found a dress that was only half ragged and helped me into it. The chest was too big and the material heavy. It left it hanging shamefully low. Then there was the hem. It was too long and threatened to trip me with every step.

Her anger radiated to my scalp as she braided my hair. Every now and then she scoffed and said something in her native tongue. I was pretty sure she was calling me names and sulking in general. Once pleated, she wrapped the braid around my head. It looked like I had a halo of sorts. I'd never worn it in such a style, so I was mesmerized by my own reflection for a moment. I was so distracted I almost didn't notice the delicious scent that was filling the house.

Was someone cooking something?

That was when the knock sounded at the door. We both turned and stared.

"What? Very busy in here!" Truth shouted.

The door opened and Ozias perched in the doorway. A large bunch of flowers were bundled in his hands.

"Sven said flowers are important." His brows were lifted, and he had this quizzical look in his eye.

I started toward him, but that damn hem tangled with my slipper and I ended up taking a spill right into his arms. He managed to save both me and the bouquet.

"Thank you." I flushed, taking the flowers from him.

I held them to my nose and gently inhaled. The fresh floral scent was amazing, I really was a simple girl at heart.

"Does that mean you're ready?" he asked, in a tone that was just loud enough for me.

The question made me freeze. No. I wasn't ready, but I didn't have time to waste. My father was a prisoner, it was my duty to make whatever alliance necessary to get him back on the throne. I slowly nodded and reached down for his hand. I figured I may as well, before he snatched a hold of my wrist again.

He led me outside, and much to my surprise, the warriors that had raided

Frankfort were all gathered in the yard. On a spit in the distance, a hog was roasting, and women were gathered in circles dancing and chattering.

It looked... normal. A few of the women drew close and reached out to touch me. They were just being friendly, but my awkwardness toward embracing just wouldn't allow it. Especially with my nerves all riled up as they were. I stayed close to Ozias's side and tried to keep a friendly smile in place.

These were going to be my neighbors. My community. Then it hit me, Ozias was in charge here... these were my people. No wonder they were so affectionate and eager to get a glimpse or graze my arm.

He didn't look like a ruler. He wore a pair of britches and a simple white shirt. He didn't even have shoes on his feet.

"Bring the priest," he called.

A woman with tattoos on her face came forward with a bowl of white paste. She smeared it down the bridge of my nose and placed a few dots under my eyes.

"Get away from her," the Cardinal demanded. "Get that witch away from the Princess!"

I doubted that the supposed 'witch' understood a word he had said. She painted Ozias's face, spoke a few words over us, and stepped away. Sven reached out and shoved the Cardinal between his shoulder blades, sending the poor man hurling toward us. He managed to catch himself on one knee.

When he tried to stand, Ozias grunted and leaned toward him, bullying the Cardinal into staying where he was.

"Say your piece, Priest." Ozias's words sounded like a warning.

They stared at each other for a long, awkward moment, then Cardinal Tullini crossed himself and started the ceremony with the usual opening.

He called on the Father, the Son, and the Holy Spirit. I couldn't help but wonder if they had anything to do with this, but I'd never admit as much. I smiled and fought back tears at times. This wasn't supposed to happen. Now I would be his to do with as he pleased. He'd fill me with his seed and I'd die in my birth bed just as my mother had before me. I started to shake and sniffle. Nothing on Earth could have moved me, but I was terrified beyond belief. I could scarcely focus on what the good Cardinal was saying.

"Highness..." he encouraged, instantly causing me to blush.

What had he been saying?

"I do," I mumbled, unsure if it was that part or not.

"Highness, are you quite all right? This... really isn't necessary," he interjected once again.

"She has agreed." Ozias' voice was low and almost growly. "I, too, agree. Does this not make us married by your Christian ways?"

"Yes. Of course," Cardinal Tullini finally

conceded. "You are man and wife before both God and men."

Sven leaped in the air and came forward to clasp his brother's shoulder.

"You've done it. You've married their princess!" he congratulated.

Then he glanced toward me and the smile sort of froze. "Welcome to your new life."

I blinked as if I hadn't heard him correctly. The man acted as if I were just a decoration. He would have fit in well back home, where women and their wombs were so easily replaced.

"Let them feast." Ozias winked, his pinky poked at and wrapped around mine. In a smooth little gesture, my hand ended up in his and he led me past the house. We went down to the creek where we'd bathed the other day and then to the woods beyond.

"Where are you taking me?" I protested, growing more alarmed with each passing step. "I... I don't want to go for a walk right now. Ozias, please..."

TYRANNI THOMAS

Chapter Twelve

My words trailed off when we happened upon a tiny clearing. There between the trees was a circle of flowers. The same type that my bouquet was made of. Here and there bones were crossed and feathers were gathered. In the center, was a shiny black fur.

He paused at the edge and pointed to my feet. His own were bare, so I slid my slippers off and set a foot down on the forest floor. The leaves crunched beneath my stockings. I couldn't stop staring at the pagan circle. It felt like I was betraying all that was holy by stepping inside with him, but he was my husband now.

Ozias led me inside and sifted down to kneel in front of me. His calloused hands slid under my gown and my knees almost gave out. He hooked his thumbs into either side of my stocking and took it off my left leg. My heart started to race and I shook a little while he did the same to my right. I wiggled my toes in the fur and stared down at him with what was, no doubt, doe eyes. I certainly felt like I was in a hunter's crosshairs.

He was in no hurry. The man ran his hands down the back of my legs and cupped my calves. He leaned back and stared up at me with his haunting green eyes and then leaned forward and planted his face in the waist of my dress. He nuzzled around, causing his nose and face to rub against places that no one had dared ever touch. His breath was warm and his hands gently clenched and unclenched, massaging my muscles in a way that conveyed his need. The dress was juggled and lifted, until he was sprinkling kisses under my navel and along my nether curls.

His lips pressed against my forbidden folds and I shot my hands down to the back of his head for leverage. I seriously thought I was going to topple at any minute. His hands slid up to the back of my thighs and he speared his tongue between my folds and flickered it against my flesh.

"Ozias," I hissed, half scandalized.

His hands found my hips and he jerked me down a top him. His mouth was on mine before I could utter another word. His hands were so needy and rough, but his mouth was soft and loving. He sprinkled kisses along my jaw and throat while his hand roamed my leg. He cast it aside, making me stretch a little further to straddle him. Without taking his mouth off me, his thumb split my folds and locked against my nub. He started to roll and crush it while his tongue parted my lips and tried to dance within my mouth.

It was sinful. It was splendid. It was so much at once. His mouth. His hands. The hardness in his pants that was pressing against my bare bottom. I'd been so concerned with avoiding a baby, that I hadn't put much thought into the act of making one, or what it would be like my first time. He was a heathen. A giant of a man. My mind started to race, right along with the throbbing between my legs. Each beautiful stroke of his thumb made my hips jump and dance. I couldn't help it; I was dragging myself along his shame and breathing heavily. My muscles started to tense and I began to grind against his thumb, helping him box that little bundle of nerves until I cried out a top him. Everything became overly sensitive, I tried to shut my legs and twisted a bit, but Ozias held me firmly in place. His wrist teased against my folds, and I heard the strings of his pants being undone.

The man was so muscular, he didn't even set me aside, he just lifted up and worked his britches off his hips. I didn't dare look down. I was terrified I'd pass out if I saw what he intended to put inside me. My mind had conjured up the worst possible images.

"Oz...," I started to whisper, on a wave of fear.

His lips found mine again and something hard and hot pressed against my entrance. I mumbled a few maidenly concerns against his lips, but they were unintelligible for the most part and did little to deter him. The hand at my hip started pulling me down and he shifted his hips, thrusting himself into me.

I scrambled to hold onto him. Wrapping my arms around his neck, I began to whimper softly. There was so much pressure and tenderness. I closed my eyes and focused on the slow circling of his thumb. The yearning, throbbing feeling was starting to come back. I made myself focus on it until my pulse was pounding in time with his hips. It was different, climaxing with him inside of me. I could feel the greedy pull and grip of my walls and the desperate way he buried himself within me before his hot seed flooded my womb.

Tears ran down my face. Not because it was ugly or because of anything he had done. I knew it was all downhill from here. I had done it. I'd signed my own death warrant. I'd be in the ground within nine months, I just knew it.

Ozias's breath fanned against my forehead as he gently shushed me. Those large hands spanned my back and rubbed empathetically.

"I hurt you?" He sounded pained.

I shook my head, sending a river of tears toward my ears.

"No."

"Then why the tears?" he asked, trying to capture some with a crooked finger.

"I'm scared," I admitted.

"'Scared?'" he repeated, "The scary part... it's over..."

I shook my head and placed a hand on my stomach.

"The birth bed took my mother. Someday it will take me, too."

He shook his head and his features pinched as if he were offended by my even suggesting such a thing.

"No. You will see the birthing bed many times," he insisted, "We will have many healthy sons and we will raise them together."

It was a beautifully painted picture, but it only served to make me cry on his chest again. He didn't seem to mind; he held me and wiped my tears like he had all the time in the world to do it.

Chapter Thirteen

We spent the night in the forest and woke up a tangled mess. His leg was thrown over me and his huge arm held me tight. It might have been nice if I wasn't naked. I'd never lain like that with a man. While he snored in my ear, I tried to search the surrounding area for my gown without moving. I just wanted to locate it and have a plan. I wanted to get dressed before he had a chance to see me in such a state.

I probably laid there blushing on his arm for the better part of an hour before I finally stretched and reached the gown. While he blinked in confusion, I shrugged my way back into the oversized frock.

"What's going on?" he sleepily mumbled.

"Nothing. It is morning, we should rise." I nodded, encouraging the idea.

He yawned and stretched without a care for his nudity. While I combed my hair with my fingers, he rolled from the ground and went to relieve himself. It was peaceful in the forest, perhaps the first night that I'd fallen asleep without listening to Truth moaning and panting.

Truth!

"You promised that the slave would be dismissed once we were married," I started, only to be met with a groan.

"She will be," he promised, though his voice said otherwise.

"You promised," I reminded him.

"She will be!" he repeated with a bit of scorn in his voice.

He did a jig into his pants and then held his hand out to help me to my feet as well. His long black hair was loose and he kept having to throw it from his face while he was bent toward me. He must have sensed my hurt, because the minute our eyes locked, he drew me into a hug.

"Truth belongs to Sven now. I will make it so," he quietly soothed, his hand slid down the back of my head and stroked my back. "All will be well, you will see."

"And my father…?" My voice cracked.

"Your father will be free," he agreed. "Soon. Very soon."

I wrapped my arms around him and held him tight. I wanted so badly to believe him. When he started to lead me back toward the farm, I gave his hand a squeeze and walked proudly beside him. It had been done. He was my husband now and forever.

Sven was sitting out back, starting his day with a jug of whiskey. I wrinkled my nose at the smell and paused when Ozias did.

"Truth is yours now," he informed his brother. "A gift."

Sven looked between us and smiled.

"'A gift?'" Sven repeated, with a soft shake of his head. "Truth is a headache and we all know it, but I will take the girl off your hands."

"You're a good man," I spoke before Ozias could. "I appreciate you; I really do."

It was easy to say. He'd found the Cardinal for me, surely that would play a big role in the recovery of my father. The way he looked at me, however, almost made me want to take it back. That antagonizing smirk and knowing gaze was enough to make anyone livid.

"I am," he agreed, standing up from the porch.

He waved the bottle at his brother and Ozias took it. He hauled from the whiskey and tried to pass it to me, but I shrank away. It was far too early to be drinking. The sun was only just starting to warm the frost from the earth in places.

"Ozias!" a voice I didn't recognize howled from a distance. His name was the only thing I understood, save for the urgency in the voice. A man topped the hill and ran as fast as he could toward us. Ozias hurried to meet him and they started speaking quickly in that foreign tongue. As they talked, they continued toward us. The more the man spoke, the heavier Ozias's brows grew with anger.

Sven had been listening intently. He grabbed the door and started to rush off into the house, but Ozias caught him.

"No. You stay with Lita," he told his brother, before walking past him. Ozias emerged a moment later with a large axe and shield.

"What are you doing?" I demanded.

When he started off the porch, I jogged right alongside him.

"Go back to Sven," he ordered.

"What? No? Not until you tell me what is going on."

"King William has reneged on our agreement." Ozias huffed, his green eyes were brilliant with rage. "He has invaded the towns along the river, land that he clearly gave to me and mine."

"I'm coming with you," I announced.

"No," Ozias said, without slowing a bit.

I scrambled to keep up with him; when the stranger brought him a horse, I grabbed his leg and prepared to climb up behind him.

"I said, no!" Ozias barked, staring down at me.

He'd never struck me, and yet I cowered.

"Go back to the house with Sven," he said, his voice was gentler, but it was clearly strained for patience.

Sven was already at my side, taking me by the arm like an errant child.

"I have her, brother, go," he encouraged.

"No," I pleaded.

What if he got hurt? All the possibilities were too much. My father depended upon him; we didn't have time for skirmishes over land. Let William have the land and rescue my father while he is distracted with his conquest.

"Why are you staying? Aren't you his backup? Surely, you are his second in command?"

"I am," Sven confirmed.

"Then who is that fool he is riding off to die with?" I berated.

"I suppose you could say he is the third."

"Well, if he is only third then he is not the best. Ozias needs the best at his back. My father…" My voice broke and the tears poured.

They didn't give a damn about my father.

Chapter Fourteen

Frankfort was a large county. The river pretty much divided it in two. It was a four-day ride to my father's castle from North Frankfort, which meant it was at least two to the river. Two days there, two days back... It had already been two weeks; how much longer would I be waiting to save my father? He could die of blood loss, be executed, or any number of things.

All I could do was wait. Wait and wonder. It seemed that was a woman's lot in some circles.

I didn't like it one bit.

"Come away from the window," Sven called from the kitchen table.

He was hunkered over a bowl of stew and staring at me. I knew he had been; I could feel his eyes. They were as palpable as the raindrops that occasionally splashed off the windowsill. My knuckles and sleeve were half damp, still I couldn't tear myself away. It had a perfect view of the hill and I'd been watching for Ozias since the sun came up.

"Young love," Truth scoffed.

"Mind your tongue, woman," Sven warned.

Truth glared at the back of his head, but she didn't utter another word.

"There!" I shouted, seeing something move in the distance.

I ran toward the door with Sven hot on my heels.

"Where?" he demanded, looking out toward the horizon.

Whatever it was that I had seen was gone now. I felt like a fool. My cheeks reddened and my heart sank. I'd been so relieved for that little moment.

"Why you pretend to care for him, anyhow, hmm?" Truth finally exploded.

She had a knife in her hand and pointed it

at me while she approached.

"You come and you change everything. Ozias dances for you, and you don't even appreciate," she accused.

From seemingly nowhere, Sven backhanded her, sending the slave sprawling on top of her own weapon. She shakily managed to pull herself to a sitting position and fumbled around the front of her gown in search of injury. There was no blood, so I assumed the knife wasn't in her. Sven kicked and sent the knife flying, confirming my suspicions.

Truth placed her hand on one of the chairs and moved as if she intended to find her feet. Sven pounced and grabbed her wrist. Truth began to scream and flail, but his grip was fierce. He held her like that with one hand and reached to his belt with the other. He had a small axe with a shiny edge that he placed just beneath her knuckles.

While Truth cried out and began to beg in their heathen tongue, Sven rocked his axe back and forth atop her fingers.

"Sven, stop!" I panicked.

It wasn't deep enough to sever them, but he was quite convincing, and the slave was left with considerable cuts to the tops of her fingers when he shoved her aside and fixed his gaze on her.

"If you ever touch or threaten to harm a free woman again, I will cut your fingers off one by one, do you understand me?"

Truth was hunkered on her knees and holding her hand. Tears flowed down her cheeks, but there was still a dangerous gleam in her eyes.

"Come." He cocked his head. "Let us find some wine and bread."

I couldn't take my eyes off Truth; I just edged my way around her and followed him. I was sort of afraid to upset him. I sat down at the table and he gathered the bread and the bottle. He kept looking at me every now and then with a bit of concern ebbing into his features.

"Are you all right, Lita?"

He said my name with an accent that caught me off guard. I stared at his lips until he squatted down in front of me and took my chin in hand.

"You're pale, are you all right?"

"Hmm?" I shook my head only to nod a moment later. "Yes, yes, I'm fine. I think I just need a short rest is all."

"You know I did her a favor, right?" He cocked his head and remained in front of me, preventing my leaving or rising from the chair. "If she so much as raised her voice at the wrong free woman she might be put to death. She was wielding a knife…"

"Yes." I agreed, unsure of what to say. "In my kingdom, anyone who draws steel on royalty would likely find the same end."

He nodded and stepped aside, bringing an arm out to support mine, his other hand found the small of my back. I was too afraid to naysay him, I let him walk me to the bedroom door like that.

"How much longer? Do you think there will be word, I mean?" I started spewing questions before he could walk away. He seemed protective, maybe that meant I had his favor and he might confide in me. I'd seen the men stopping by now and again.

"I do not know. The only thing that is certain, is that fighting has commenced. Wounded men have been brought home. Others have been recruited in their stead."

"How many?" I blurted out.

"How many what?"

"How many wounded men? What do the numbers look like?"

I was no war genius, but I knew a little, from all the days of playing in the castle halls. I was an ever-curious child and loved to listen in on my father's council meetings.

"I'm riding out in the morning," he admitted.

My heart pounded and my world spun a little. What did that mean?

"Get some rest, we will talk when you wake."

There was no resting. Who could have slept after news like that? He'd just made an even further enemy out of Truth, and now he was going to leave me with her. Even more, Sven had been taxed with looking after the women, and now he was being sent for. Surely, that was not good news. The numbers must have been depleted.

I tossed and turned, trying to clear my mind and think of a way out of all of it. A solution that would see me to safety and my father set free.

A short time later, the door slammed and a fight broke out. Truth and Sven were both shouting in their native tongue. It sounded like a herd of elephants had been let loose. Things were being broken and someone was being slammed around. I nearly broke my neck trying to leap from the bed and get out there.

The minute I opened the door, I was met with the barrel of a pistol.

"Stop," Sven demanded in perfect English.

The man behind the gun shoved me back into the room, sending me sprawling across the bed.

"Stop, she is your princess."

The man lowered his gun and reached his hand out toward me.

"Princess Lita?" He asked.

I recognized his bright-red uniform as my father's and nodded my head. The soldier stared at me for a long moment, then his face contorted. Before I could scream, he brought his pistol down on my temple and the world went black.

Chapter Fifteen

Truth's manic laughter brought me to. That and the bumpy cart ride. I was tied at the wrist and feet. I struggled to get up and managed to rock myself into a sitting position. We were in the back of a cart with bars all around the side.

"Let me out of here at once," I demanded.

"You'll be out soon enough, Princess," a soldier sneered.

"Too funny. Now you are a captive, too." Truth winked.

"I have been a captive since I laid eyes on you," I reminded her.

She snorted and looked at the men riding on either side of our cart. They were armed and keeping a close eye on the three of us. Sven had a wound on his head that was slowly leaking blood. His eye was swollen and he was coming in and out of consciousness.

The ride was long and miserable. Sven woke up a few hours later. All he could do was groan and shield his eyes from the sun. I helped lug him into a sitting position so that he wasn't staring directly up at it. He didn't help much at all and he was so heavy. I tried my best to keep him propped against my shoulder.

It lasted for a while, but after another few hours, my back grew stiff and I had to shrug him off. He groaned again and grabbed his head. By then, the sun had set, not that that slowed our pace any. The men marched and carried us through the night.

I tried to sleep, there was nothing else to do, but my anxiety and the rough ride wouldn't allow it.

"The river," Sven whispered, the following morning when we stopped alongside it. There was no fighting. There wasn't a soul out there, besides us.

"There is a bridge half of a mile down river," one of the soldiers reported.

Thus began the long haul of steering our cart along the river bank. The wheels got stuck twice and the horse spooked over a frog. I thought for sure that we would die before we ever got to the bridge.

Once we made it across, it was like we'd entered a whole new world. My father's banners had been replaced at the manor houses we passed. The town entrances had white and gold flags now. It made me tear up at how easily their loyalty had been bought.

By the time we arrived at the castle, my bottom was sore. My lower back was bruised in places from being jarred against the cage and my neck was so stiff. I could definitely tell we'd been at it for four days. Alas, the cart rolled in front of the gate and a flock of soldiers hurried outside. I recognized one or two of them. It was easy to tell which had been my father's, they avoided all eye contact and hurried to do their duty and get away.

Sven was dragged in one direction, and Truth was hauled off the other way. They took their time getting me out of the cage. I was carefully carried and placed on the ground at the bottom of the staircase.

"You could at least help me to my feet," I grumbled to one of the men who was trying to pretend that we didn't know each other.

"I can't," he whispered, after a time.

"His Majesty, the King!" a voice called from the top of the stairs.

I looked up in time to see William in all his white and gold glory, descending the steps. Behind him, Cardinal Tullini kept pace with a perfect scowl.

"I was robbed a wife." He laughed. "The country's queen stolen before she could even utter her vows."

"Stop it," I demanded, when I realized he was jesting at Brianna's expense. "You're a vile man. A coward!"

"I'm your king. Soon, I will be your

husband."

I took a lesson from Truth and spat directly in his face.

"You are dead, you just don't realize it yet," I assured him.

His smile grew tight and someone ran forward to dab at his face with a cloth.

"Her Highn… I mean Lita, here, has already taken vows," the Cardinal spoke up. "She is married to a heathen."

William laughed like it was the funniest thing he'd ever heard.

"She can't marry a heathen. Pagan weddings are not recognized by myself or the church."

I didn't give a damn about anything the Cardinal had to say. Their words were just background noise to me. I wanted to claw the Cardinal's eyes out. He was always a nuisance, but this was too much. This was treason. He'd betrayed my father, his people, and now me.

"There is a special place in Hell for traitors like you," I promised him.

"You see, listen to her filthy mouth," the Cardinal protested. "She's been with the heathen's far too long."

"She's my only option," William abruptly turned and hissed at the Cardinal. "You yourself have counselled me on such matters."

"That was before I knew that she had stooped to such disgusting ways," Cardinal Tullini protested.

"There are those in the kingdom who would rebel. I will stifle any such thoughts by marrying their princess." William all but dismissed the Cardinal, placing his icy gaze and attention solely on me.

I shivered and suddenly understood why Brianna had begged not to marry him. He had beautiful blue eyes and shiny black hair, but the man was a monster. A murderous monster. And now, I was fated to take him as a second husband.

Chapter Sixteen

William escorted me to my old chambers, taking care to walk shoulder-to-shoulder with me, without making any effort to handle me. He opened the door, and I was greeted by a small group of maidens.

"Your ladies in waiting," William explained.

The man's smile spoke of how generous he felt he was being. I was no fool, though, I knew they were his women. Their loyalty was already bought and paid for. I wouldn't trust any of them, I could scarcely be bothered to keep track of their names.

There was Petra the blonde and Contessa with the exotic traits and smokey eyes. He'd probably already laid with half of them. The rest were the doe-eyed, 'new to court' variety that fell for everything that afforded them a smile.

Ruined women, every last one of them.

"Well, I'll leave you ladies to it." He clasped my shoulder and my stomach churned. I thought I might be sick right there on his shoes. Once he left, I sat on the edge of the bed while Contessa scrubbed my nails and Petra took down my hair. A few of the sturdier girls brought in a washtub and filled it with water and flower petals.

"I don't like rose water," I protested.

Contessa chuckled, and tapped my hand like she was scolding me.

"You just trust us, Highness. We know what King William likes."

I sighed and shook my head, causing Petra to pull a strand of my hair.

"Enough." I drew my hands toward my body and shook my head free. "Out. All of you."

I shoved my finger toward the door and bugged my eyes until they reluctantly left. I rubbed my temples and tried not to think of my immediate future. I had to focus on my father. Where was he? How many men were secretly still loyal to him?

"Psst," a voice called, from behind the door.

It was so quiet and random, that I jumped in response. A chill ran through me and I stared at the large oak door.

"You are not alone, Princess. All is not forsaken."

I sucked in a breath and raced for the door. When I opened it, there was no one there. I looked up and down the hall, but it was empty. I was barefoot and my hair was free and dangling down my back. I didn't give a single care. I marched down the hall, fully prepared to investigate. A set of spears crossed before me and I jumped back with a gasp.

"Sorry, Princess," a soldier with hazel eyes apologized. His tone was deep but earnest.

"Go back to your room," the man on the other side demanded.

"Did someone—?"

"Go," the hazel-eyed stranger growled.

My footsteps echoed as I tore off back to my room. I really needed a bath, but I didn't want to do William any favors, and I certainly didn't want to draw his attention or earn his affections.

I was so close to my father. He was somewhere here in the castle. In the tower, I was certain the Cardinal had said. I sniffled and contemplated the whole mess of it. Who knew if Ozias was dead or alive? I felt a little bad for him, he had been loyal to me, even if I was his captive. He'd been gentle and good to me, even providing me with a Christian ceremony.

Before I knew it, the tears started again. I wiped them aside and got into the tub while the water was still lukewarm. I sat there until I pruned and then scrubbed my hair in the cold. I couldn't even get dressed; once I got out, the chill forced me in front of the fire. That was where I sat until one of the ladies in waiting knocked on the door. She didn't wait for permission to enter; she opened the door just enough for her to slip inside and closed it behind her.

"Your... Forgive me, Mistress, but I don't know your title?" She was a cherub-faced girl with kind eyes.

"I am the wife of King Ozias. That makes me Queen Lita or Majesty," I proudly informed her.

He had said there were three kings, but I'd never cared to acknowledge such until now. I took a deep breath and pulled the towel a little tighter around me.

"Oh, Majesty!" She hurried forward. "Let me dress you, please?"

She nibbled on her lip and studied me with the most empathetic gaze.

"Alright," I hesitantly relented.

She beamed and went to my wardrobe. It felt like so long since I'd had one that I was speechless. I just stared at all the fitted clothes and fancy shoes.

"Perhaps a lilac-colored gown, if I may?"

the lady offered.

"What is your name?" I asked, once I'd given a nod of consent.

"I'm called Lucille," she meekly answered.

"Were you at court before William...?" I thought better of my words and let them trail off.

"My grandmother and mother before me were cooks in your majesty's kitchen before King William's reign," she cautiously answered.

"Cooks?"

He had the daughter of a cook serving me. No wonder she was constantly looking around in awe.

"How did you come to obtain this position?" I probably sounded rude, but my curiosity got the best of me.

Her cheeks colored and she looked to the ground.

"I've lived with heathens, child. You can speak plainly with me."

"My mother." She sniffed and colored a bit more. "She bore William a son."

I wasn't expecting that. It immediately knocked any spite out of me.

"I, uhm... I'm sorry to hear that." I wasn't really sure of what to say when one confided that they had a royal bastard.

"Please do not dismiss me, your majesty. I promise I will be your most loyal servant. My mother would be reduced to begging, if anyone found out." Lucille started speaking fast, clearly having realized she'd said too much.

I placed my hand on hers and reassured her with a shake of my head.

"You're the most honest person that I've found since my return. A genuine soul."

She settled a bit but kept nibbling on her lip.

"Your mother is loyal to William, then." I cleared my throat, piecing it all together.

"Not at all. He had their baby killed so no

one would find out. He took away with one hand and gave with the other, your Majesty." Lucille quietly explained.

Chapter Seventeen

I was never left alone for long. Even when I ordered the ladies to leave, those guards poked their heads in every fifteen minutes or so. It was so hard not to feel trapped and suffocated. I paced the floors but that only made my thoughts race. I needed to have a clear mind for my father's sake.

So, I poured a bit of wine and went to the window. I could see the tower from there. Every now and then shadows shifted in the windows of the tower, but I had no way of knowing if they were his, so I didn't bother making a show.

The door creaked and I turned to find William letting himself in. His smile made me sick. How could he even look at me after what he did? The nerve!

"I've come to see that you were well handled."

His words were met with silence, it was all I could do to control my facial features, I couldn't form a response.

"I know, I know, you've been through much in the past weeks." He brought his hands out as if I actually intended to interrupt him. "But that is in the past. We are of strong stock. We can overcome this tragedy and any other that life throws at us. Together, we can do it all."

His voice lifted and fell, emphasizing the parts he wanted me to focus on. He truly thought my intellect inferior, that I would be steered into having some type of feelings for him.

I wanted to murder him in his sleep. In fact, I suddenly realized that I welcomed the opportunity to do so.

"Yes," I agreed, "the past."

I swallowed hard and tried to hold onto my temper.

"We need to forge a new tomorrow," I kept it just as poetic as he had tried to.

"The people need to have direction and reassurance that their country is no longer in turmoil."

"That's right. That's the spirit!" William came forward and embraced me. "I knew you were the bright one of the bunch."

He smelled of harsh soap and cheap ambition. He'd fought and now I knew, he still hadn't won my father's people over. If he had, he wouldn't need me. Those were the things I focused on, rather than the arms around me. I hated hugs, each time I got one it took me back to the loss of my mother. It was a maddening test of my resolve, but I managed to give a few pats to his back before I leaned away and stared up at him. I placed every effort into a youthful, hope-filled smile.

"I always pictured a wedding in the gardens." I licked my lips to wet the lies that kept on spilling from them, "Do you think it's large enough?"

"The garden…," he repeated, before looking toward the wall in a thoughtful manner. "Yes. Yes, I can see it now. We shall have some roses brought in, a mixture of your house colors and mine. A new reign..."

The sin in his eyes made my stomach flop and my mouth salivate. I had to get away from him. Fast! I scampered toward the window and got sick over the balcony ledge.

"Princess?" William asked, coming out toward me.

"Highness," someone cautioned from the door. "She must be examined. We must make sure she is well before you get too close. She may be contagious with some Heathen disease."

William withdrew his hand and stared at me. Then he hefted his shoulders back and walked toward me. His hand found the small of my back and he rubbed it tenderly.

"Nerves?" he asked.

"Mhm," I lied, wiping my mouth on the back of my hand. A servant hurried forth and cleaned my hands with a warm wet cloth. I couldn't help but color at my own manners. "Forgive me."

"Nonsense," William's rubbing turned into a reassuring pat. "It is natural for a bride to have nerves. We will marry in two days. I don't want the anticipation to overwhelm you."

"In two days…" I gasped, right along with the Cardinal.

"Indeed." William nodded to confirm it.

"Sire, will that not leave the country men whispering over her honor?" the Cardinal carefully ventured.

"It is not just the country men." I spoke as if possessed, offering my enemies political advice. "You would risk being ridiculed abroad. The other diplomats…"

"The other diplomats be damned." William scoffed. His face reddened and he let go of me and started to pace.

The Cardinal and I glanced toward each other and William exploded.

"What then? What would you have me do? I must act or these same foreigners will look at me as a rebel... A cause that should be snuffed so they can go back to predictable old Charles."

I curled my toes and inwardly cursed him and his line for generations to come. Then I realized I was doing so and felt bad about it for a moment. It was surely an offense to think such things. I'd go to mass later, for now, I had to step in before the Cardinal picked up the reins.

"First you must give the illusion that all is well. That a peace has been sued for."

"A peace sued for?" the Cardinal stuttered and finally spat.

"Indeed. His Majesty must convince the people that my lord father sued him for peace. Make it known that I was his offering. His only remaining daughter offered up to you and the people."

"Yes," William sank his teeth into the fabricated victory. "Yes, we must make preparations."

"Charles will never—!" the Cardinal bellowed.

William turned on him and placed a hand on his sword, sending the Cardinal stumbling backwards several paces. He was a robust man and fell backwards in the process.

"You will ruin it all!" the Cardinal hissed before running toward the door.

"How do I get your father to go along with this?" William asked, turning his attention on me.

I swallowed hard. It was a gamble, I'd probably be seen as a traitor if word ever got out, but I'd give anything to see him. The opportunity to get him safely out of that tower was worth a thousand weddings. I alternated between that and the silly notion that Ozias was still out there somewhere.

Perhaps I was betraying both him and my father. I could only pray they'd forgive me.

Chapter Eighteen

The next evening, the servants came bustling through with a tub of water. Behind them, each of my ladies carried expensively wrapped gifts. They lined up one-by-one in front of me. Lucille stepped forward and unwrapped the parcel she'd been charged with. As the paper fell away, I was presented with my old golden tiara. It had been a gift from the queen of Spain. The front had little sapphires and white diamonds in it. That particular tiara had always been my favorite.

The next three girls presented me with the matching jewelry.

"How sweet, his first courting gifts are the items he stole from me," I mused under my breath.

Lucille blushed and smiled, clearly fighting off her amusement. She seemed to have been the only one close enough to have actually heard me.

When the last of my ladies stepped forward and unwrapped my mother's ruby and onyx crown, my hands shot over my mouth. I hadn't realized he had the crown jewels.

I mean, of course, he had them, but I wasn't thinking about material things. I'd been worried about my father and our people.

"His Majesty hopes that you will enjoy these gifts as he's so graciously presented them. He asks that you wear them and join him and your father for dinner tonight."

"Dinner with my father..." I couldn't even fathom.

It was a wonderful notion. One that made my heart swell and my mind race, but part of me had come to know men and their games. I assumed it was a trick or something that I'd be expected to pay for later. It didn't matter. There was nothing I wouldn't do to see my father again.

I stepped toward the last girl and took my mother's crown from her. It felt heavy despite its delicate appearance. I placed the crown on my head, but I didn't feel any different.

"Majesty," Lucille gasped, "Majesty, it's beautiful."

The other ladies sighed and admired me. One brought the mirror forth so I could see myself properly. I looked like her. My eyes were a bright green from all the tears. It was the only time they got that brilliant hue.

I tipped my head up and stared at the woman in the mirror. The person I'd become. My smile and eyes were different. Sharper. Knowledgeable.

I could do this. I could match this pretender at his own game.

"Bring me the red and black evening gown and set up my cosmetics."

They eagerly did as I asked. The ladies in waiting might not have been ladies at all, but they were the closest thing I had to company, so I tried to make the most of it. Their names were coming easier these days. The lot of them prepared my bath and left me to enjoy it for a few minutes. When they returned, Petra helped me into the gown while Contessa and a girl named Susette powdered my face and lined my eyes.

Just as Lucille was starting on my hair, there was a knock at the door. I gave Petra a nod and she hurried over to answer it.

The Cardinal's ancient voice impatiently boomed, "Open, child."

"Leave it," I commanded under my breath.

They all burst out in giggles, causing the man to further anger.

"In the name of—" he started, just as Petra threw the door open.

"Cardinal Tullini." She feigned surprise and quickly stepped aside.

"Lady Lita—" he began, raising his hands up in that way that he was prone to do when he wanted someone's full attention.

"Majesty," Lucille corrected

He glared at her before sniffing and fixing his gaze on me once more.

"Let it be known that if you disappoint the king tonight, I will personally let you burn. I know this is a ploy. It is unwise to let you rendezvous with your father, but the King will not be..." He was so busy rambling and talking with his hands that he didn't see William enter behind him.

"The King will not be what?" He spoke up, in a way that begged for confrontation.

"Sire..." the Cardinal stuttered.

"Indeed. Please continue... The King will not be what?" William refused to budge.

"Sire, I have tried to reason with you..."

"I'm not a child to be reasoned with, priest." William's voice dropped low and menacing.

The ladies all went quiet, some even placed their hands over their mouths when

William pointedly rejected his title.

"I will have my bride, I will have my country, and I will have your obedience as well." He inhaled through his nose dramatically and placed an arm around my shoulders.

"You look stunning." William purred in my ear. "Never mind this old fool, he clearly has had too much to drink at such an early hour. Are you quite ready, Princess?"

I reached up and felt my hair, then gave a nod. It didn't matter if it wasn't entirely finished, he'd promised a visit with my father!

I was getting so good at performing for him, that I wrapped my arm around his and accepted his escort to the dining room. I even smiled a little when I felt him looking my way. From the corner of my eye, I could see his triumphant expression. It sickened me, but I managed to continue the charade and gave his arm an affectionate pat.

I felt good about things. This was the beginning. The first few sacrifices that would see my father on his throne again. We rounded the corner into the dining room and my heart dropped to my stomach. At the far end of the table was a man in rags. His long, once-regal hair was now matted and greasy. The hem of his pants stopped inches above his ankle and his face was dirty.

"Father...," I whispered.

He didn't budge. His hair continued to hang about the table with his head bowed. I shifted, to go toward him, and William placed his hand on my arm to stop me.

"Please," he moved to the middle of the table and pulled out a chair, "maintain your distance. He is still a prisoner of the state."

"A prisoner..." I shook my head in denial. "That won't do."

Somehow my voice found a spine and I made certain I held his gaze.

"The father of the queen cannot be a prisoner," I lectured. "The entire illusion that you are trying to weave for the people will fall to ruin. Do you want it said that he gave you the kingdom or that you usurped it like a common thief?"

Chapter Nineteen

William stiffened and then sniffed dismissively.

"In time, Highness. All in good time. We have much to discuss."

He patted the back of the chair, encouraging me once more to sit. It took everything in me to keep my eyes on him and not run to my father. I mechanically made my way to the chair and sank down in it as gracefully as I could muster.

It was so different from North Frankfort. The rich tablecloth and expensive candles were things I'd forgotten about. I tried to focus on that instead, but it only made me realize that I missed Ozias. I couldn't help but wonder where he was. Perhaps he was dead, or maybe he would kill me for betraying him with William. I grabbed for the wine and sipped the sweet, dry brew. I could feel William's rich, blue eyes on me, so I pushed the thoughts away lest I become tearful. I suddenly got hit with all these emotions and a terrible bout of nerves. My hands shook, so I clasped them. I didn't want William to decide I was too overwhelmed to visit my father.

"Father, it is good to see you," I whispered, causing the old man to lift his head.

Tears glistened in his eyes, but he held them in check.

"I'm sorry," he mouthed, inaudibly.

That damn near broke me. He was betrayed. Robbed. He had nothing to apologize for.

"Charles, you'll be pleased to know that I have recovered your daughter from the heathens. I saved her from a dirt-poor pagan life. She could have been a farmer, but no... she will be my queen." I couldn't tell if he was trying to gain my father's favor or rub it in.

My nails bit into my palm so hard it made half-moon marks. I tried to keep my eyes forward, looking at the guard rather than William or my father. It was easier to address him, he was a faceless man, hidden away behind a metal helmet.

"William stole me from a man named Ozias. He has made an offer to allow your freedom in exchange for my hand."

"I would rather die of seclusion and starvation," my father growled.

He'd looked too weak to even be able to speak and yet William's news had rallied him. His eyes were sharp and piercing. He was a prisoner sitting at someone else's table and yet, he might as well have been back on his throne. There were some things you didn't acquire with a crown; my father had the heart of a king.

"Such could be arranged, but I'd much rather you not—" William started.

"I'll not have you kept prisoner," I cut him off and stared down at my father.

I sat up and made sure that my chin was parallel to the ground. "You are a giant amongst men. A natural ruler and my father. I cannot be free and live my life while you are locked away to rot."

He heard me, I knew he had, but his gaze grew distant. His thoughts clearly grew thicker as the silence spanned.

"Let us eat," William bid to the servants.

I drew my shoulders back, but said nothing as a bowl of soup and a spot of bread were placed before me. The cup bearer scrambled forward and replaced the sip of wine I'd taken. He was a young boy, perhaps ten or twelve. His hands shook and I watched as his eyes shifted but never actually set upon me.

"What is your name, boy?" I asked, without thinking.

He froze and lifted his innocent, pale-blue eyes.

"My name is Victor, if it pleases you, Highness." He bowed his head in a practiced way and attentively stared at the floor.

I reached out and placed a finger under his chin, lifting his wee face.

"You look so familiar."

He had a cherub face and the softest voice.

"I am a brother of Lady Lucille, Highness," the boy confided.

"Ah. Yes, my most favored lady in waiting."

I knew what it meant to have the queen say such a thing. The girl's family's place and power in court just increased tenfold. She deserved it. She'd been my only friend in this horrid place that I'd once called home.

The boy beamed with pride.

"Off with you now. Give your sister my best if you see her before I do."

I glanced back to the table and found William glaring at me.

"Are you quite finished?" he asked, looking between me and the retreating Victor.

"Yes."

"Good. So, Charles the Fallen, your daughter and I will be married on the morrow. I expect that you will be there, looking supportive as ever. You will nod and clap when she is crowned on the following day. If you fail to do so, I will publicly execute you both."

He nodded, and a set of guards came forward. My father looked like he hadn't eaten in days. His food had scarcely found his plate and they were hauling him up by the arms. It took everything in me to remain calm and stay quiet.

I just needed a day or two. I had to figure things out.

Chapter Twenty

"Do you think that, perhaps tomorrow I could have a supervised audience with my father?" I cleared my throat and asked, once he'd been removed from the dining room. The guards had escorted him in chains back to his tower, all but breaking my heart.

William studied me with an odd smile.

"For what?"

"I just wish to hug him and tell him that all will be well. He must embrace this new reality. I do not want anything unfortunate to happen to anyone." I tried to act the role of a sovereign compliant bride.

"Yes. Yes, that might prove beneficial," he agreed, before picking up his spoon and starting in on his soup.

He slurped on the spoon in a way that

grinded my nerves. My father's stomach was probably chorusing with hunger and here he was behaving like an ill-bred child. Each bite he took was accompanied by moaning and slurping. One would have thought he'd never had a cooked meal before.

Alas, he sat his spoon down and I followed suit, grateful to be dismissed.

"My compliments, it was all wonderful," William told the servants.

Meanwhile, I glared at them for not putting poison in it. I'd have gladly sacrificed myself along with him. If it put an end to all this madness, I'd do it. The scorn must have crossed my brow, the servant reaching for my bowl paused midway and jerked her hand back. I scooted my chair back to give her room and she finally took it.

"Will you see me back to my room?" I asked, trying my best to convince him that I actually looked forward to such a sign of favor from him.

"Absolutely." He stood and moved around the table until he was pulling my chair the rest of the way out and offering me a hand. I took it and gracefully rose from the seat. He walked so close to me it was almost obscene. His hip brushed mine with every step and at times his hand ventured to the small of my back. I wanted so desperately to sprint ahead, but I had to play the part.

My king and country depended upon it.

When we reached the door to my chambers, he shifted and placed himself between me and the large oak door. His hand found my jaw. The man's touch was so tender I jerked away from him at first. He wasn't to be denied, though. He darted his head forward and brushed his lips against mine.

"Sire!" I beseeched. "I am not your bride yet. Such displays are inappropriate."

"Is that what you told King Ozias?" he whispered, not allowing me to back up an inch, he followed my every step until the wall caught my back. I was effectively pinned with him in front of me. His hand settled on my waist and I stilled. "Tell me, did you lay with that heathen?"

I knew better than to answer. Any answer would be the wrong one.

"Well?" he barked, growing a bit red in the face.

"My father promised me that I would never know men or be forced to produce heirs," I cried, and tried to bring my hands up to cover the tears that had suddenly sprung forth.

I feared he'd hurt me or force me into a situation, instead he smoothed his robe and jerked his head toward the doorway.

"Off with you," he scoffed, with a disgusted look on his face.

For once, I didn't sass or even respond, I just scurried behind my chamber door and lent my weight to it while the tears openly poured. I'd failed his test; I just knew it. Now he knew that my heart truly wasn't in it.

What if he didn't let me see my father?

What if he went back on his word and decided to leave him in the tower despite it all? A sob caught in my throat and my knees buckled. I was so tired; I was truly exhausted in my heart and my soul.

"There, there, Majesty," Lucille comforted.

I was startled, not realizing anyone was in the room. I was still used to my private time back at home with Ozias and Sven. She sank right down on the floor with me and patted my shoulder. I was so relieved that she didn't try to hug me. I tilted my head so it rested on her shoulder. Just being in the presence of a kind face did wonders. It had been so long since I called anyone friend, I supposed Lucille was as close as it got.

"You miss your father, huh?" she guessed "You weren't gone long. I imagine it was painful to see him taken back. I'm so sorry, Majesty.

I nodded and the tears started to seep again. I tried to keep my eyes closed, as if my lashes could dam the tears, but they didn't.

I surrendered to the darkness, and awoke to Lucille gently shaking me.

"Majesty," she bid. "Majesty, you must come quick."

I sat up straight, my heart was pounding, "What is it? What has happened?"

She put her finger over her lip and waved me onward. I followed her to the door with confusion written all over my brow.

"Now," she urged. "Before the guards return."

I flew after her. She took me to the council room and started to shove on a closet door. It sounded ancient when it finally budged and scraped across the stone floor.

"This is the tower passage," I blurted out.

I recognized it from tales alone. "They have taken cardinals and nobles alike through here to put in the tower or perhaps meet the axe-man over the years."

Lucille went pale.

"I had heard rumors but I wasn't sure if it

truly existed until you went to dinner. That is when I came down here and investigated," she admitted.

I swallowed hard. There was no going back, if I was found they'd probably put me in there with him. So, I watched her grab a candle and then I hurried inside and helped her pull the door shut behind us.

Chapter Twenty-One

The tunnel went beneath the moat, so it was damp and cold. Our steps echoed, and after a time, my anxiety grew so bad that I was certain someone would hear us coming. Everything that could go wrong was going through my head.

"Wait," I whispered. "We snuck past the guards at my door, what about the tower guards?"

"I met one earlier." She swallowed and looked at me. "I promised him that I'd come back and see him after dark."

"You what?" I stopped walking altogether and gawked at her in disbelief.

"It is okay, Majesty. It is my duty. To you and the King." Loyalty shone in her candle-lit eyes and she set her jaw. It didn't stop her lip from quivering, though. Before I could say otherwise, she hurriedly took a few steps forward.

"We must hurry, Majesty, before the other ladies ask after you."

I knew she was avoiding any more talk of the matter, but I couldn't argue her point. So, I quickly followed her.

"Are you a maiden?" I asked, unable to drop the matter.

She lifted her chin as if I had insulted her.

"I am, Majesty."

"And you would risk your future, any chance at having a decent husband?" I whispered.

"If it restores my king to his throne, I would lay down my life," Lucille confided, "The truth is, I enjoy his company. We normally meet in the garden, but I... I wanted to kiss him under the stars, Majesty."

Her loyal words and youthful dreams gave me strength and warmed my heart. It also distracted me from the many spider webs. When we reached the end of the tunnel, another large door lay in wait. I started to shake a little and my stomach churned.

"Here we are." She put her ear to the door and we stood there for what felt like an eternity. "Okay. Wait until you no longer hear anyone and then slip upstairs. You will have to find him on your own from there."

I nodded in understanding. She gave my hand a squeeze and then let herself out, leaving the door slightly ajar.

"There you are," she quietly greeted.

"Indeed. It is me." A masculine voice laughed.

I heard what sounded like footsteps and then Lucille gasped. They noisily kissed for a few seconds and then scurried off down the hall.

I waited a bit longer and let myself out.

The moonlight seemed so bright after being in the tunnel. I kept the candle with me and hurried across the opening to the stairwell. The shadows played off of it as sconces flickered and crackled along the wall.

I made it to the second floor of the tower and held my breath while listening for signs of life behind the heavily enforced door. I heard nothing, so I climbed a bit further to the third floor.

I heard breathing on the other side. The prisoner within groaned in pain while the aged boards of his bed creaked. It broke my heart to think of his old bones sleeping on that miserable bed.

"Father?" I whispered against the door.

I held my breath, and the silence spanned. A shuddered breath sounded from behind the door and then a muffled sob.

"Now I am hearing things, oh, Lord," he mumbled.

"Father it is me, Lita," I hailed on another whisper. "Come to the door, Father."

The sobbing stopped, and after a moment, I heard shuffled steps approaching.

"Lita?" he quietly cried.

"Yes, father." I had no way to get inside. I placed my palms on the door and rested my forehead on the rough wooden surface.

"You mustn't be here, they will execute you, too." He panicked.

"No one is getting executed." I tried to shush him, but he gave another shuddered breath.

"He will make you watch, Lita. You must be brave."

"He won't. He wouldn't do such a thing. He has promised me that you will be free once we are married. He insists that I marry him," I rattled, a little louder than I intended.

"I know. He promised me that I would live long enough to see you married," Father quietly confided. "He said that you would be forced to see me be executed. He intends that his wedding gift to you will be my head."

"It will be a quiet affair and the public will

be told that he has retired to live out his days in the country," William finished from behind me.

I nearly fell up the stairs, I turned so abruptly. He had Lucille by the hair. Her mouth was gagged and tears streamed down her face.

"Let her go," I demanded, while standing to face him.

"Oh no." William laughed. "She is willing to lay down her life for her king, remember?"

My heart fell to my stomach and flipped so fast I thought I'd be sick.

"No matter, I will only require that she lay down." He motioned to the guards, and they carried Lucille past me.

William stepped around me, just as I heard Lucille's clothes being ripped.

"I trust you can see yourself out," he condescended, before heading up to join them.

"Lita," Father hissed. "Lita, I beseech you,

leave. Leave while you can, that girl is at their mercy, and you will be, too, if you follow them."

I curled my fists and closed my eyes. Rage and terror collided. I didn't make him any promises. I couldn't walk away and leave her to those animals.

"Wait. No, please!" Lucille screamed.

The men's laughter answered her.

She cried out in pain and I tore down the stairs, unable to bear the sound of it. I made it halfway down before guilt caused me to stop again. What was the worst they could do to me? Nothing that wouldn't be done the minute I became William's bride. Would he really share me with all those men?

Familiar blue eyes silently studied me from the first room I'd passed.

Sven!

He didn't say a word, he just watched me and then shifted his gaze back up the stairs.

I weighed the possibilities and then tiptoed back up them. They had left the door open, not an ounce of shame between the five or so men. Directly in front of me, a guard had his pants lowered beneath his bottom. He was bent over the top of Lucille, forcing his tongue in her mouth while he ground his hips against her.

She was kicking and squirming, it was obvious he hadn't managed to impale her yet. They smelled like a brewery. A few others were standing around the room encouraging him. Some were occupied with their cocks in their hands, others were simply staring.

I had no idea what I would do, I couldn't stop staring at the man's bare bottom. Then something caught the moonlight there on his belt.

It was a dagger!

I darted forward as quick and quietly as I could, grabbed that dagger from his belt and sank it into him where his neck met his shoulder.

He howled in pain, and I whirled, catching a second guard in the chest. The other two and William stared wild-eyed. William's hands came out before him, like he was trying to reason with me.

"Lita, put down that weapon. It is a crime to pull a weapon in front of your king, woman," he reminded me.

It was too late to back down now. The first man I'd stabbed was gurgling and dying near my feet. The other was leaning against the wall while dark blood leaked from his uniform top.

"Leave me," I demanded. "Go back the way you came and we will pretend this never happened."

Lucille wept behind me.

"These men will escort you to your room," William agreed, "And we will act like none of this happened."

The soldier's head spun toward William in disbelief.

"Go," I told him, taking a half-hearted

swipe at his stomach. He jumped back and waved his arm, inviting me to pass him. "I'm not stupid. You two go first."

"Go, I will stay and guard the king," the other uniformed man told him.

"Lita," William called, as we were filing from the room.

I turned and a shiver ran down my spine when I saw the evil in his dark-blue eyes.

"We will be married at dawn."

Chapter Twenty-Two

I didn't sleep, I just couldn't. There were only a few hours until dawn. Lucille was still shaken-up. She was almost inconsolable.

"How would you like a nice hot bath? I could summon a servant?" I offered.

She shook her head and swiped at the tears in her eyes. They were puffy and her voice thick with emotion, "No, Majesty. It isn't that. You saved me from anything too... horrible."

"Then what is it?" I pried.

"It's just that... he is so evil and come tomorrow, you will be exactly where I was tonight." Her lip trembled and the desperate tears came again. "He will punish you for all of this, and we are helpless to stop it."

"I don't expect you to stop it. It was my agreement with him. My father's freedom, for my hand."

"He doesn't intend to free him, though, Majesty," Lucille gently reminded me.

I stared blankly at her. My denial was so thick that I could do nothing but blink.

She sprang from the floor and took a shawl from the bed. Without being asked, she wrapped it around my shoulders and settled onto the bed beside me.

I couldn't think and yet I had to stay focused. One step at a time or I'd unravel at the seams. Falling into despair would have been so easy to do. I couldn't allow that. I'd figured out what to do in Lucille's case, something would come to me to save my father, too.

It had to.

I pushed my shoulders back and marched toward my wardrobe. I found a beautiful blue gown and grabbed my favorite crown. When I put my stockings on, I took a ribbon and fashioned it around my thigh. It served as a perfect holster for my new dagger.

"What are you doing, Majesty?" Lucille gasped, when I turned around to face her. "You have to run, Queen Lita. You must!"

I shook my head and took her cherub cheeks in my hands.

"All will be well." Perhaps it was the denial talking, but I said it all the same.

"Get yourself freshened up. Get dressed," I encouraged.

She shook her head, "I have to go, Majesty. They will come for me, when you are occupied."

She didn't owe me a thing, and yet, I felt betrayed that she would leave me. I hadn't left her. I stayed and I came to her aid when needed.

I told myself I was being unreasonable. I couldn't ask someone to subject themselves to rape and beatings on my behalf. She still had a swollen lip from last night.

I started to tremble and her hand found my arm.

"Please, I implore you, Majesty... Come with me?"

"I will do what I can to help see you safely out," I assured. "But I cannot leave my father. He will certainly kill him if I am not here to intervene."

"My Queen, you have no means to plot an intervention. There are those loyal to your cause, but they are afraid of William and too few in numbers."

I raised my hand, bidding her to silence as my father often did his subjects. I had made up my mind. I would stay.

"Get the water pails and tell the guards you are preparing my bath. When you get to the courtyard, don't stop. Don't look back, just get yourself to safety." I made her promise.

She swallowed hard and nodded her head. Her bottom however, did not leave my bed.

"Lucille...," I gently started, "It is now or never."

The shadows were thinning outside, soon William's men and the Cardinal would be coming to escort me to the royal chapel.

She strangled a sob and rose to fetch the pails. She gave a final look over her shoulder, tried to brave a smile, and quietly let herself out.

My only friend was gone. I truly was in this alone. I almost felt defeated, but then I thought of my father and knew I couldn't give up. He wouldn't give up on me.

I went to the mirror and started applying my cosmetics just as Petra rushed inside.

"Highness, forgive me." She flushed and begged. "None of us knew that your wedding would be so early and sudden."

"Neither did I." I weakly smiled.

She attended to my hair as the other ladies started to arrive.

"Where is Lucille?" Petra asked.

"I have sent her on errands," I lied.

"Step aside, young man," Cardinal Tullini's ancient voice commanded outside my chamber.

He didn't knock or even call out; he threw the door open and bellowed from the entrance.

"Hurry up, child. We don't have all day."

Chills ran down my spine. It seemed like only yesterday he was ushering Brianna to her death. I didn't give him time to harp or perform, I walked past him and kept my pace brisk. He struggled to keep up. Once I even thought I heard him curse under his breath.

I beat him to the chapel, and waited outside the door. I didn't know how to bring myself to enter.

"Where is my father?" I blurted out, when the Cardinal caught up.

He didn't answer me, he snatched me by the arm and opened the door so all could see us. There were twice as many people inside as there had been for Brianna's wedding.

It was the king's wedding, after all.

Most of the noblemen were heavily armed, no doubt unwilling to risk a second surprise attack. Everyone stared, some people even whispered as I walked down the aisle. There in the front row was my father. He looked at least ten years older than when I last saw him, and it had only been a few hours.

I swallowed my emotions and forced my shoulders back. I kept my chin up and I marched toward my fate. The dagger teased my thighs, almost begging to be used. I knew that I'd never be able to sink it in him. Not here with so many guards anyhow.

The whole chapel went quiet when the cardinal stepped to the altar and started praying in Latin. I should have been paying attention to him, instead, I kept stealing glances of my father. I desperately wanted to go to him. To hug him. Something I never wanted to do.

The bells rang a single time and the people outside cheered the start of our impromptu wedding. The roosters hadn't even crowed, and peasants were gathered to celebrate this façade? It puzzled me.

"Princess Lita," the Cardinal hissed, drawing my attention back to the matter at hand.

I blinked and it was like coming out of a dream. When my eyes opened, the door splintered and Sven stepped inside. Ozias's men filed in after him.

I cried out, in disbelief and joy when Ozias limped behind them. He was injured, but it didn't stop him from raising the business end of his axe and pointing it at William. Tears streamed down my eyes. The nobles drew and Ozias's men started swinging.

"No!" I shouted. "Lay down your weapons, these are the men of King Charles."

The room stilled and my father rose.

William lunged for me and I squatted and shot my hand under my dress. When he came at me again, I brought the dagger out and buried it in his gut just as Ozias sank his axe into the pretender's back.

Blood splattered and stained my pretty blue dress. It shocked me. I stared at the ugly, crimson stain. When I finally snapped out of it and looked up, Lucille was standing in the doorway.

Ozias wrapped me in his arms and planted a kiss on my forehead. I wrapped my arms around him and held on for dear life. I didn't want to ever let go.

"Good people of Frankfort," my father called, in a shaky voice. "Hail your future king and queen."

Ozias lifted me off my feet, and I swatted at him.

"You're injured, put me down," I protested, but he insisted on carrying me down to my father.

"King Charles." He bowed, and spoke in that slow broken way of his. "I want you to know that I care for your daughter. I will protect and love her. Always."

"That is all I could ever ask." My father smiled.

While Ozias held me in his arms, I leaned out and wrapped my arms around my father's neck. It was all I had wanted to do, ever since I thought I would lose him.

Chapter Twenty-Three

In the days that followed, I could tell that the ordeal had taken its toll on my father. He was slower and smiled less often. When he did, it was usually toward me and Ozias. They'd grown quite close, both of them excellent with strategy, they would talk long into the night of their old victories.

"Lita, I am happy to retire," he admitted, while we sat in the gardens. "I am getting old. The people need a protector. They need someone who is young and ambitious. It is time I passed the crown."

I licked my lips and started to shake my head. How did I tell him that I couldn't do it? Queens produced heirs and well, that was something I would not be doing. Lately, Ozias had been careful to remove himself from me each time before he finished. He truly cared for my happiness and wishes. Despite our rocky start, we were an amazing couple.

"People will... expect things from me," I reminded him, as gently as I could.

"You have a husband now, Lita. It will happen in time and when it does you will be an excellent mother."

I shook my head in denial, and noticed Ozias standing behind him.

"When is the last time you bled?" he finally spoke up, causing my father to whip around with indignation.

"Who...? Oh...," my father trailed off, the anger leaving his tone.

I opened and closed my mouth, but I couldn't speak. I'd not menstruated since I met Ozias.

He smiled back at me and rubbed his own stomach.

"It is much more noticeable to those who haven't seen you in a while," my father agreed.

Three weeks later, I stood in my red and

black dress, and let Ozias tuck my arm around his. We wanted to get the crowning over with, before I grew too large with child. Ozias and I slowly made our way to the throne room and took the path toward the dais. I'd been so nervous in the time between, but now, as the sun shone through the windows and the people smiled on us, it felt right.

Cardinal Tullini was in the tower, awaiting his trial, so a new man, Cardinal Fontaine was officiating.

He spoke fast, at times I didn't really understand all of his Latin. Then he handed over Ozias's crown and scepter. The process was repeated, and my mother's ruby-red crown was exchanged for one that was solid gold. It had been hers, too. She'd sat on the very throne I was being ushered to and she'd stared out at these same people.

Emotion started to overwhelm me. A queen was supposed to sit regally and keep her composure, so I blinked against the tears. Ozias reached over and placed his hand on mine and they quickly went away.

I wasn't around to help him learn the art of diplomacy, in the months that followed our coronation, I had to go lie in wait for our child. Thankfully, my father had no intentions of leaving our side.

I rested easy with the knowledge that he would see Ozias through it, just as Lucille would see to me and our unborn child.

"He goes to every council with the king," Lucille told me, when she came to help with my bath.

She was my only source of information, thankfully she was loyal and good at collecting details.

"The people love and respect him," she continued, while running the sponge up my arm and across my shoulders.

"As they should. He is a good man," I assured her.

"I believe you." Lucille smiled.

She helped me to my bed as she did every

night and prayed with me for the safe arrival of my child. I was so glad she had stayed. There was no one else I wanted in the room with me when the day came.

"The king was keen on being present for the birth of the child, but I think your father and the midwife have convinced him that such a thing is not proper in our customs." Lucille was practically reading my mind.

I wasn't sure what to say, so I remained quiet. The thought of having a man in the room was a little intimidating. I'd watched my siblings being born. I knew what it entailed and I didn't want him to see me like that.

I stood from the water and Lucille dried me off and led me to the fire. She had chamomile tea prepared and left me to sip it while she hunted some clothes.

"I'm so sorry, Your Grace." Lucille flushed. "I thought I had a gown laid out for you already."

She leaned over the trunk to grab a gown,

and I felt a tiny gush. It startled me. At first, I thought I had urinated, but then it kept trickling.

"Lucille…," I called in a panic.

"What is it?" She hurried to my side and her mouth fell open. "Oh, Majesty! It is time."

She helped me to the bed, completely forgetting about my gown. I supposed I wouldn't need that. I started to get squeamish about an audience, but by the time they arrived I had the worst pain in my back. I was twisting and rubbing. I'd have given anything to make that pain go away. Every time it did, however, it came back a few moments later.

"There, there," the midwife called, bustling inside. She threw my knees apart and stared at my sex. "Good, good there's plenty of time for us to prepare. Ladies, water, rags."

I glanced up and realized my ladies in waiting and several noble women had joined us. I tried to snap my legs together, but the midwife pried them open and started to check the baby. I squirmed away from her, but then another contraction hit and I groaned against it.

"The babe is swift. A strong and healthy one." She chuckled.

I didn't find anything amusing about the situation. The pain was coming so fast, that it almost felt like it wasn't stopping at all. Soon, I couldn't move around to accommodate it. I was tired and sore. There was so much pressure, I feared I would split in two.

Alas, I still suffered another hour before the midwife motioned to the ladies and they came to help me sit up a bit.

"You will push when I tell you," the midwife instructed.

My heart slammed in my chest and the baby pressed down with another round of pain. I screamed and the midwife tapped my knee.

"Now!"

I pushed and fire spread through my lower region.

"Keep pushing," she encouraged, despite the fact that I was already desperately doing so.

I fell back and cried. It did nothing to relieve the pressure.

"The baby is in your birth canal; you must push again," the midwife said, while watching my stomach a moment. Then she swatted my knee. "Again.

I screamed and pushed until the pain exploded and tiny cries filled the room. I started panting and reaching between my legs. I was terrified that I'd bleed out, like my mother had. The ladies fought to keep my hands back.

"Your Majesty, the after birth must come," a lady explained.

"I don't want to die." I sobbed.

"What? Your Grace, no," the midwife assured, while someone swaddled the crying infant and brought him to me. "You are fine. Your son is healthy and you will go on to bear many more children."

The woman might as well have threatened me. If I had the energy, I'd have probably tossed her out right then and there. Before I could do so, Lucille placed the babe in my arms and all hostilities were forgotten.

Ozias came bursting through the door like he was preparing to make battle. His smile was so big.

"You did it!" He laughed. "You did it, Lita."

He came to my side and leaned over to see the baby. I was aware people were working between my legs with the after birth or whatever they had called it, but I didn't care.

Nothing mattered save my new family. I looked into that boy's eyes, and suddenly it was all worth it. The pain, the tears, everything I'd gone through meant nothing.

I wasn't a captive, I was captivated.

ALSO, BY TYRANNI THOMAS

RH

The Thorns and Thrones Series
Of Princesses and Pawns
Of Sovereigns and Savages
Of Coups and Cauls

The Heathen Harem Tales Collection
Keeper of the Norns
Between Mortals and Makers

The Krypt Series
Chasing the Night
Taking the Night
Light up the Night

The Crossroads Priestess Series
The Crossroads Priestess

Captivated

Midnight Miracle

Sin Eater

The Soiled Dove Series

Soiled Dove

War Whore

Natural Born Sinners

The Hunger Saga

The Hunger Saga

Blood and Betrayal

HISTORICAL FICTION

The Scars Series

The Scars of Survival

Wearing the Scars

HISTORICAL ROMANCE

Highland Secrets

TYRANNI THOMAS

Highland Honor

Keepsake

No Mercy

About the Author

Tyranni Thomas is a former nurse with a love of all things Heathen and historical. A writer of High Fantasy Reverse Harem, Historical Fiction and LGBT who believes that written words speak louder than most people's voices ever could.

TYRANNI THOMAS

Printed in Great Britain
by Amazon